Not a Chance

NOT a CHance
JESSICA TREAT

FC2
Normal/Tallahassee

Published by FC2 with support provided by Florida State University, the Unit
for Contemporary Literature of the Department of English at Illinois State
University, the Program for Writers of the Department of English at the
University of Illinois at Chicago, the Illinois Arts Council, and the Florida Arts
Council of the Florida Division of Cultural Affairs.

Address all inquiries to: Fiction Collective Two, Florida State University,
c/o English Department, Tallahassee, FL 32306-1580

For more about Jessica Treat and other FC2 authors and books, visit our
website at *http://fc2.org*

My Friend George
Words and Music by Lou Reed
(c) 1984 METAL MACHINE MUSIC INC.
All Rights Controlled and Administered by SCREEN GEMS-EMI MUSIC INC.
All Rights Reserved International Copyright Secured Used by Permission

ISBN: Paper, 1-57366-089-2

Library of Congress Cataloging-in-Publication Data

Treat, Jessica, 1958-
  Not a chance : stories and a novella / Jessica Treat.-- 1st ed.
    p. cm.
  ISBN 1-57366-089-2
  I. Title.
  PS3570.R359 N68 2000
  813'.54--dc21

                                        00-009717

Cover Design: Polly Kanevsky
Book Design: Tara Reeser

Produced and printed in the United States of America
Printed on recycled paper with soy ink

This program is
partially sponsored
by a grant from the
Illinois Arts Council

Acknowledgments

Stories in this collection first appeared in the following periodicals and anthologies: "Ants" in **Black Warrior Review**; "Walking" in **Epoch**; "Not a Chance" in **Hawaii Review**; "Dead End" in **Unhinged, a Magazine of Disturbing Fiction** (UK); "Nicaraguan Birds" in **Web del Sol**; "His Sweater" in **Dominion Review** (*Dominion Review Fiction Award*, 1996, judged by Ben Marcus); and "Radio Disturbance" in **Green Mountains Review.** Sections of the novella, "Honda," first appeared in the journals **Chiron Review, Seattle Review,** and **Writing Women** (UK), and in the anthology **Chick-Lit 2: No Chick Vics** (Fiction Collective 2).

With gratitude to Rilla Askew and Shira Dentz, trusted friends and readers, for their understanding of my work and their comments— incisive, invaluable—at nearly all stages of story, manuscript, book. Thanks also to Jonathan Baumbach and to Peter Bricklebank for their help in shaping this collection. For help with technicalities y detalles tecnicos, *thanks to Kathie Fox and Bessy Reyna. Grateful acknowledgment is also made to the Fundación Valparaíso in Mojácar, Spain, for granting me the time and space to work on some of these stories, with special thanks to Martha and Morten Keller,* directores extraordinarios. *Finally, my thanks to Henrik Haaland—.*

Contents

ANTS

1.

My boyfriend used to eat ants. He told me that and I can see him: kneeling in a corner of their summer house (it is France) where the plaster wall crumbles. Ants are racing furiously below the window where the sun streaks through and Marc attacks them eagerly: one, then another, another one. He has four, now five in his mouth. They squirm on his tongue, tickling the roof of his mouth before he swallows them. It is this sensation that makes him eat them everyday in the summer, one summer after another. It is his secret activity, his secret pleasure, until his father finds him.

"Are you eating those things? Good God!" And he grabs his arm, pulls him away from the window, the sun, the ants who are now darting in all directions at once.

He is taken to a doctor. Marc sits on a chair, legs dangling, while the doctor (white coat, round glasses) faces him.

"How long have you been eating ants?"

Marc looks down at his hands. He twists his fingers together.

"You don't know?"

He shakes his head.

"How many did you eat?"

He is afraid to answer. He knows he can never count them.

"One? Two? Eight? Ten?"

"Five," he says. It is how old he is.

"Why did you eat them? Did you like how they tasted?"

He doesn't know the answer. He's never asked himself before. How they taste? They taste bitter; they almost sting him.

"Don't your parents feed you enough? Don't you like the food they give you?"

The questions continue and Marc nods his head to them, knowing only that his one pleasure has been stolen; he'll never have it again. Except … maybe if he's careful, while they're all playing gin rummy at the card table in the garden, when they're looking down at their hearts and spades; he could sneak away, into the house, the room…

The doctor is staring at him. Marc feels his face reddening. He wipes his nose with his sleeve. He'd like to cry now, but he won't, not in front of the doctor.

He is taken to a white room, told to lie down on a long bed with a machine over him. A light stares down at him, so hard and bright he wants to shut his eyes and never open them. He wonders what it's doing to him—is the machine changing him, making him never want to eat them again?

"You can sit up now," a voice tells him.

His mother and father are waiting for him. They look down, their eyes scanning his as they take him by the hand. He smiles hesitantly, his eyes full of doubt, as he looks up at them.

A few years later it happens. He feels it like the afternoon sun through the window. It warms him from his forehead to the soles of his feet, sits soft and glowing in his belly: something will happen to him. Something large, larger than himself, than his parents, than his sister even. It scares him some, but he knows he can do nothing to stop it. He won't try, but he won't encourage it either. It will happen anyway, no matter what he does.

He stores his secret. Even to think about it might hurry it somehow; he is in no hurry. He will wait as long as he needs to, even longer.

Sometimes he feels it in his stomach like things racing there. He remembers the ants he's eaten and wonders if any are still alive, squirming inside him. Is that what makes him feel funny? He eats something to stop the sensation, to slow the squirming; he chews on his shirt collar and bites his fingernails. He chews gum and then the wrapper; he eats his father's cough drops and searches the cupboard for chewable vitamins and aspirin. Most of all he likes the aspirin. He fumbles with the lid; his hands are shaking. Years later he will be looking through the spices in my cupboard for something to add to his omelet. He'll open the jar marked cardamom and the smell will remind him: it is the smell of children's aspirin. He'll put it in the omelet, the one he is making for me that I can't eat; the spices are overpowering. "But Caroline," he will say, "I made it for you," and the hurt in his voice, like that of a child's, will almost make me.

2.

He is sixteen when he meets Georges who is nine years older than he is. Georges is his tennis instructor. Marc hates his sculpted calves, his hard chin, the sand-colored hair in a V down his chest. He himself is thin, bony-kneed, a body like a bird's. And Georges is always picking on him. He corrects Marc more than anyone else, even though

Frédéric has a serve that's much worse and Alain can't seem to hit the ball.

Once Marc sees Georges with his girlfriend coming out of a restaurant in St-Germain. He's dressed in a white sports jacket and his hair is slicked back. He nods at Marc, a sharp shake of his chin, but Marc pretends he hasn't seen him.

Sometimes on the court he feels Georges' eyes on him and everyone else disappears; there is only the space, a few feet, between them. Marc feels his heart beating too fast, trapped inside his rib cage. He fumbles for a cigarette.

"When are you going to give that up, Marc?" Georges asks and reaches for the pack, but Marc pulls back from him. There is a tennis ball at his foot; he picks it up and flings it at him. The ball catches Georges by surprise; it hits him on the chest where the cross hangs on its gold chain, but Marc doesn't see this; he's turned and started to run.

He hears his name being called but he won't look back. He leaves the *lycée*. He'll go home. But it's too early. He's still in his tennis clothes. He should go back to the gym. He doesn't want to run into anyone, doesn't want to be seen. He walks home, throwing stones as he goes.

"Fucked up asshole," he says to himself with each stone that hits the pavement. "Shit-face," as they skid under cars. He lights a cigarette, inhales deeply; his hands are shaking.

But the day comes when Georges dismisses the class, "Everyone can go now but Marc—Marc, I'd like to talk to you." Marc feels his face whiten, his heart thudding inside him. Surely the others know? What is Jean-Paul thinking when he looks back at him just as he's leaving the room? But they all leave. No one comes back to save him; no one tells him it doesn't have to happen.

"Marc...," Georges almost whispers his name. Georges, always so blunt and commanding, suddenly sounds gentle. But Marc can't look at him. He looks down at his feet instead. His legs are melting. There's nothing there to support him. He's falling, but Georges has stepped forward and catches him; Georges is holding onto him. Marc knows this is what he's both hated and wanted, but a larger sense of relief floods him, diluting his fear, as Georges hugs him harder.

Georges and Marc are inseparable after that. Georges has his own apartment and Marc spends evenings there and sometimes weekends, when Georges isn't with his girlfriend. His girlfriend must know about them, but she doesn't let on if she does.

They wake up together and drink coffee in bed and Marc introduces Georges to Lou Reed and cocaine and Georges says nothing about his constant smoking. They play tennis together. Vacations they go skiing in the Alps. The whole of St-Germain must know about them but Marc no longer cares. Georges does though. Maybe because he's older, maybe because he has a girlfriend. He gets angry at Marc when Marc takes his hand as they walk down the sidewalk, when Marc grabs his ass, when Marc makes a scene in a restaurant. Because Marc is always making scenes. A waiter who keeps removing plates before they've finished infuriates him.

"Why don't you take my underwear too while you're at it?" Marc says and then can't stop laughing.

Georges looks away from him. "You're such a child."

"Just how you like them," Marc says and Georges throws his napkin on the table and walks away. But Marc has no money. Georges comes back to pay for the dinner, walks out again.

"I don't give a shit," Marc says aloud. He eats slowly. He can't finish the veal. The waiter avoids him. He leaves the restaurant. He looks for Georges' sports car. It's not there of course. Marc decides to walk to his apartment. He'll apologize. But not again. He's sick of having to apologize. For what? It's not his fault Georges cares so much about appearances. Marc cares only about Georges and himself, and sometimes his sister Murielle, sometimes his mother.

He has a limited amount of caring. Later it will be only for me and himself, he'll tell me that: "You're the only one I care about, Caroline, the only one I love," and for a long time I'll believe him.

3.

It's his parents' 25th anniversary. His grandparents, all the relatives are there. He and Murielle have finished the punch bowl. They get high in her bedroom. "I'm gay," he tells her and she says, "I know."

"Do Mom and Dad know?"

"No, but I'm sure they're wondering."

"Well I don't want them wondering. I'm going to tell them. I'm telling them right now," he says, getting up off the bed, checking the mirror before he leaves the room.

"You can't do that! You're crazy—*mais tu es fou!*"

But Marc is already on his way to the living room.

"I have an announcement to make! Quiet everyone!" He sees his parents exchange glances.

"Well, let's hear it!" his uncle says, "I'm all for announcements."

Murielle is holding onto his arm, "Don't do it!" she whispers.

"Leave me alone," he says, shaking her off him. "Listen, everyone…"

"Well, out with it," his father says.

Marc takes a deep breath, "I'm a fag! " And then in a louder voice, a voice that screeches out of him, *"Je suis pédéeee. I'm queeeerrr!"*

No one says anything for a moment and Marc goes to the punch bowl for a glass. His mother blocks him. "How can you say that? Apologize! I demand an apology! Here, in front of everyone!"

He tries to get around her and hears his grandfather's deep voice, "Well, so much for the family lineage…."

"How can you do this, and on our anniversary?" his mother continues, while his father, drunker than Marc, eyes him coldly.

"He was always a difficult child," his grandmother is saying, "and the only boy in the family…."

"I don't give a shit!" he shouts and feels the room reel, spinning under him.

That's all he remembers from the party. At some point he calls Georges and the phone seems as if it will never stop ringing. At last Georges answers.

"I told them, I told them about us."

"You what? You—to who?"

"I told my family I'm a fag!" Marc shouts into the phone, and Georges says, "Boy, you've really lost it," and hangs up on him.

It's never mentioned by his family. Sometimes Marc wonders if it really happened, but he can remember the room right before he spoke, how it felt to have everyone watching him, waiting for what he would tell them, how for a moment the whole world was under his spell. And Georges forgave him even if his parents never really did. He and Georges have laughed about it since. Even now they think it's the funniest thing he's ever done, wonder how he ever found the courage, though courage is also stupidity, Georges has said.

4.

Georges is going to get married. He hasn't said so, but his friend Pierre let it slip, on purpose probably. But Georges himself says nothing. Sometimes when they're alone together, eating in a restaurant, Marc can see Georges wants to tell him. He watches Georges clear his throat, fiddle with his napkin, and waits. He pours more wine for both of them. Georges brings the wineglass to his lips, puts it down again. It's coming now, Marc thinks.

"You know Marc, I was thinking, we could spend a weekend in Paris. We could go to a rock concert."

"Sure, when?"

"Oh, I don't know, maybe next weekend…."

Georges is stalling. They go to Paris, buy more records, crash out in a friend's apartment. Marc snorts heroin at a party. He's sick the next day; he collapses on the sidewalk. Georges carries him upstairs to the apartment. He changes Marc's clothes and lies beside him while he sleeps. Every few hours he takes Marc's temperature and rubs his sweat-soaked body with alcohol.

"Marc, I was so scared. You could've died…," Georges says when Marc finally opens his eyes.

Marc smiles at him. "So what if I did?"

Georges stares at him.

"Georges, don't leave me," Marc says, and Georges buries his face in Marc's body.

Marc wonders if Georges hasn't changed his mind, if maybe Pierre didn't make it up after all.

One Sunday they're driving back from a tennis club. All day Georges hasn't said much of anything. He keeps his eyes on the road and only says "yes" or "no" to Marc's questions.

"It's really a thrill to be with you," Marc says finally. "You're so communicative, there's so much to talk about."

"There is something to talk about," Georges lets out in a tight voice. "There's something I have to tell you."

Marc waits and hears, "In August I'm getting married."

"I know," Marc says.

Georges stares at him, "You know? How long have you known?"

"About four months."

"Who told you?"

"Pierre did."

"So you've known all along, you've sat there knowing and knowing, just waiting for me to tell you—"

"More or less," Marc says.

Georges pulls off the road. He looks over at Marc who returns his gaze. Marc feels the old hatred surge up inside him and he wants to hit Georges, to pound him on the chest, to cry out at him.

Georges reaches past him to open the door. "Get out. I don't want to see you anymore."

"Whatever you say," Marc says, hesitating for only a second before stepping out of the car and onto the side of the road. Georges drives off, pulling the door shut as he goes.

Marc picks up a rock and hurls it. "Fucked-up asshole," he says. A car passes him before he thinks to stick out his thumb. And then he sees Georges' white sports car coming toward him. It makes a U-turn and pulls up beside him.

"C'mon, get in. I'll drive you home."

"No way."

"Marc … I'm sorry." Marc sees that his eyes are red. "Just get in the car, don't make it hard for me."

"I'd rather walk," he says. "Anyway, you're getting married, remember?" He slams the door which Georges has opened for him and walks away. He waits for the sound of Georges' car behind him and doesn't hear it for a long time, and when he sees it drive by, it's only a white blur disappearing.

He doesn't talk to Georges again. Once he is sitting on the balcony of a café with Murielle when they see him. They stand at the rail to watch him. He looks older, thinner.

"Why don't you talk to him?" Murielle asks.

"He's a jerk, you don't understand," he says. He lights a cigarette, smokes it quickly.

They sit down to eat but the sight of the soup makes Marc feel sick. Murielle is saying something to him. He lights another cigarette and chews on his thumbnail.

"Let's go now," he says.

"But I haven't finished. We haven't gotten our main course yet."

"I don't care. The food sucks. I'm getting out of here." He leaves her in the restaurant.

He walks as far as the field at the edge of St-Germain. He sits down to smoke a joint. He wonders why he's still living if everything he's waited all his life for has already happened.

5.

"How long have you been shooting heroin?" the doctor asks.

"What?" Marc says, "I've never shot myself up with anything."

"How many times?" the doctor insists.

Marc remembers a different doctor. "How many did you eat?" How many had he said? Five? Six? But there had been hundreds.

"You don't know? Too many to count? You can't remember?"

"I told you," he says. "I'm not an addict."

The doctor writes something down on his clipboard.

"What are you writing?"

The doctor doesn't answer him.

"I'm a queer, not an addict—why don't you write that? Why aren't you writing it? Write it down: first-class queer!"

The doctor is eyeing him.

"Go on! What are you waiting for?" Marc shouts at him. He sinks back into the pillow. He's breathing hard; his face is red. He closes his eyes. He thinks he hears the doctor scribbling madly on his clipboard, before sleep overcomes him.

He learns from Murielle that Georges also has it: Hepatitis, Type B—drug addicts and homosexuals. The only two cases in the history of St-Germain. Marc smiles to himself. "My wedding present to you, Georges," he thinks. In some way it marries Georges to him.

But the doctor insists Marc is an addict.

"I've never shot myself up with anything!" Marc tells his parents, but he can see they don't believe him. Even

Murielle seems doubtful. Why? Because Georges is going to be married? Because they can't imagine men fucking? Who are they trying to save?

He gets lectures from his mother, "It's all those drugs, they've changed you, you're hardly like the son I've known, not my son...."

"Well, you're not like my mother," he says.

She ignores this. "God will forgive you. God will set you on the right path again." She takes his hand. "I'm praying for you," she says.

He gives up trying to defend himself. He's weak; he's lost twenty pounds already. He doesn't care anymore. "I hope I die," he says.

Murielle asks what she can bring him. He asks for books by William Burroughs and Yukio Mishima. She brings him a Walkman; he listens to Serge Gainsbourg and Lou Reed. The songs depress him. There is one, "My Friend George;" it was their song. *I knew George since he was eight / I always thought that he was great / And everything that George would do / You know that I would do it too....* He stops the song, buries his head in the pillow.

6.

He hears about Georges' marriage: Georges looking barely recovered, pale, too thin. His sister says she's seen him. He looks awful. Good, Marc thinks. But he can't stop remembering.... He feels confined in this house, this town; everything tastes bitter to him.

Murielle is going to marry her boyfriend. Marc refuses to go to the wedding, saying he isn't well enough. He gets another lecture from his mother. His father avoids him. He wants him out of the house, his mother has said.

He sees Georges once more. He's walking on the other side of the street in the opposite direction. He has a new haircut but his sweater is the one he always wore. He catches Marc's eye and crosses the street toward him. Marc waits, his heart beating up into his throat. He lights a cigarette, tells himself to keep on walking. But he doesn't move. He wants to hear him say it: it was all a mistake…. He wants to hear him say it, even though it's too late. A car passes between them and Georges steps back to let it go by. Coward, Marc thinks, and turns and walks away from him.

"Marc!" Georges calls out and Marc glances back, but he can see Georges has nothing to say to him. He walks faster, flinging his cigarette as he goes and Georges doesn't call out again. Someone told him that Georges' wife is pregnant. Well, now he's got everything.

He doesn't see Georges again. The baby is a boy. He'll tell me they name him Marc, but a moment later he'll deny it.

7.

It's a city no one knows him in. There's an ocean to separate him from France, Georges, his family. He has a room in a small hotel in the Centro, a place for prostitutes, he thinks. He can imagine Burroughs staying in such a room; it reminds him of the room where Lee of *Queer* lived. During the day he wanders around. He doesn't know Spanish. He eats in American-style restaurants, where he can look at the pictures and know what he's ordering. He learns some Spanish from studying the menus.

The Vips on the corner of Reforma and Florencia, he's noticed, is favored by gay men. He likes to watch them: Mexican men with skin the color of café au lait, neat moustaches, tight buttocks. They probably go home to wives and children. One of the men catches Marc staring at him, gives Marc a wink, but Marc looks away from him, feels his face burning. The faggot, he thinks.

In the Librairie Française he meets Valerie: tall, blue-eyed with short blond hair and just as new to Mexico; Marc falls in love with her. "You're like a brother," she tells him. "We're like family, why do you want to change that?" He wonders if it's because she's taller than he is, because she finds him feminine. He's not feminine; he's more a man than the rest of them. He wants desperately to make love to her. He's only done it once with a girl and that was when he was much younger. He has to know if he likes it. But Valerie refuses and Marc knows he'll lose her if he keeps asking. And then Valerie tells him her friend Etienne will be visiting on his way down to South America. Marc stops by the bookstore to meet him but Etienne hasn't shown up yet. In the evening Marc goes to Vips.

He orders what he always does; the waitress knows him now. He finishes his soup and looks up to see a man watching him. He's young, maybe thirty, with dark curly hair and a pair of glacier glasses on a string round his neck. He looks French. Marc picks apart a piece of bread and looks away from him. When he looks back the man still has his eyes on him. He knows, Marc thinks. But I'm not anymore, I'm not queer. His heart is beating too quickly. He feels sick; he can't finish the enchiladas the waitress has brought him. He puts some money on the table, takes his coat and leaves the restaurant.

He walks quickly down Reforma, takes a right on a side street, looking back once as he does. The man with the glacier glasses is there; he's following him. Marc walks faster. What does he want from him? Go away, he says as he walks, Get the hell away from me. He turns down a dark street; the street is lined with prostitutes. The man is still half a block behind him. Marc is afraid to go to his hotel; he doesn't want the man to know where he lives. But where else to go? A girl with big tits and a face with too much lipstick is staring at him. "*¿Quieres?*" she asks, leaning into him. He nods. She takes him by the arm, and Marc looks back once at the man to see him staring after him. He thinks he sees his mouth curling up in a grin.

Marc can't do it with the woman. Her mammoth breasts and her smell, pungent and salty, make him feel like vomiting. She jerks him off. He pays her; it's cheaper than dinner anyway.

In the night he wakes up sweating. He sees the man: his face was beautiful, dark and finely chiseled.

Valerie introduces him to Etienne the next day, a man with dark curly hair and glacier glasses. Marc takes one look at him and leaves the bookstore. Valerie runs after him.

"What's going on?" she asks.

Marc stares at her. Why couldn't she have loved him? "Just tell your friend to shove it up his homosexual ass," he says.

8.

If she knew his feelings for her, if he could tell her, it might be different between them. One night he decides to find her. He's wasted on coke and tequila and other things he can't remember. Valerie won't come to the door. Marc keeps on ringing. He leans against the bell so he doesn't have to keep on pressing it. At last she appears. She's in a red bathrobe. "You're beautiful," Marc says. He tries to kiss her. She draws back from him. He stumbles past her and slumps down on her couch. "Come here, *mon amour*," he says. She does at last but he's passed out by then.

She arranges his body so he can sleep and finds a flask of tequila in one pocket, a bottle of barbiturates in the other. She decides to make an appointment for him. She asks around; someone recommends a doctor in the south of the city. When he comes to, she drives him there. "His name is Dr. De Ovando," she says. "In 3F. Knock on the door, he's expecting you. I'll be waiting for you here."

Marc goes to the building she's pointed out to him. He climbs the stairs, stops at the apartment on the third floor. There's a plaque above the number. "Dr. De Ovando," he reads, "Psychiatrist. University of Mexico."

He takes the stairs down two at a time. "He's not a doctor—he's a fucking shrink!" He can't wait to give her a piece of his mind—he's ready to kick her car in. But the car isn't there.

He starts walking. He walks for blocks and blocks—where are the buses and taxis? There's dust and it swirls up with the wind. He feels it sting his eyes and settle on his clothes. Where is he? It was all a trick; she tricked him. He knows he won't forgive her. He walks blindly down streets he's never seen before. People are staring at him. He doesn't see them, doesn't see the group of children who stop to watch him as he swears in French, "The cunt, the little bitch...." He doesn't notice them but sees a rose at his foot, single and half-trampled—it's lost the stem—and he picks it up, fingering the petals absent-mindedly. A petal falls off and he puts it in his mouth and chews on it. "Is he going to swallow it?" one of the children asks and his brother nods, still staring at him, "Yes, he's eating it. He's eating a rose!" But Marc doesn't hear them. "In the end she's just like the rest of them," he says, crushing the rose in his hand as he does. They've all deserted him, every last one.

9.

He knows she's different from the rest of them. He decides this from the first, when he notices her at the Alliance where he gives French classes and then keeps running into her. He sees it when he invites her for coffee and learns that her birthday is the same as someone else's. "Who?" she asks, but he shakes his head. "Someone else I loved...." "Then you're saying you love me?" and he says it in French to her, "*Oui, je t'aime.*" She smiles at him, "You're joking of course," she says, but her eyes tell him she believes him.

He sees it when he speaks to her, the way she listens to what he says: that his girlfriend has just left him, that he's living in Burroughs' old apartment.

"This is where he did a William Tell number on his wife, you know, with a glass of gin on her head," he says, when she first visits his room.

"It is...?" she asks, looking around at all the furnishings.

"Yes, he misses the glass—BAF! He shoots her instead."

"Are you sure?" she says, and if she believes it's true, it's because by now he himself does.

Later, after cigarettes and tequila (he drinks what she can't finish), they tumble onto the couch, their legs, arms, mouths entangled, all a tangle in the pillows and magazines and ashes from an ashtray that spilled. In the bedroom they turn away from each other to undress and then she's under him, belly white and expectant, and he watches her face to avoid looking at the rest of her, and when he comes, he does it shuddering down into darkness.

He opens his eyes to find her lying on her stomach, looking not at him, but at something small and black crawling near the bed. She takes it between her forefingers and squishes it dead.

"You have ants," she says.

He stares at her. "They weren't here before," he says.

"No?" she asks.

He's looking at her still and she returns his gaze, as if she knows he has something to say and she's waiting, and she isn't going to interrupt him when he does.

WALKING

Not long ago I dreamt of him: I was walking down the street and suddenly he was right beside me. I was surprised—after all these years—but he didn't seem to be. He held my arm and laughed, before moving away again. There was a force and directness about him I hadn't associated with him. I hadn't thought of him at all until then—truthfully I'd forgotten all about him. But I began to remember: that he never wore socks, how he wore his watch around his ankle.

At the time we were neighbors. His apartment was the same as mine only backwards, a mirror image. He used to say hello to me, then stand in his doorway, awkwardly, as if he wanted to invite me in but didn't know how to. I thought him odd: besides his watch, there was his hair that stood up in the back, like he'd just woken up and hadn't brushed it properly. Still I was curious. We would stand in front of our doors, two guards who didn't know how to change places. I had a cat who would rub against my ankles and would sometimes venture over to his. It seemed to make him nervous.

"Is that your cat, then?"

He had a slightly British accent. I know I must have asked him where he was from, but his answer was evasive. Or he told me and I can't remember. There was a conversation about the Indian Ocean, a place where the warm water met cold, and because of this, there were always crazy weather patterns, constant shifting.

Did he invite me in? I seem to remember sitting at his table and drinking beer from a bottle—it was what he had to offer. Was it because I could see the unmade bed in the next room (mattress on the floor) that I began to imagine myself in bed with him? It wasn't beautiful to watch: awkward and urgent, too much like a quick hard burst to be satisfying.

Once in my own bed in the middle of the afternoon, I couldn't get the picture of him, his pale, too long body, his mattress, the two of us attached and groping, from my mind. After spending myself on him and not falling into the lazy nap I usually did, I decided to do something. I don't know why—maybe because I felt I had to get some fresh air, have it breathe sense into me—I came up with the idea of going walking. I knocked on his door, loud and hard, as if it were urgent business instead of an idle invitation. He opened finally, looking himself as if he'd just gotten out of bed (though it was after 3:00): hair standing up, shirt half-open.

"Oh, it's you...."

"Do you want to go for a walk...?" I blurted.

"What? Is it nice to walk around here, then?"

Walking was obviously a foreign occupation.

"Can we walk later? I mean, can you check back in an hour or two? We could go then."

I decided to go without him. We lived in an abandoned warehouse section. There wasn't much to see: low brick buildings, faded block lettering for tile factories, and then square lots with rows and rows of tires, used mostly. I began to imagine the barrels of chemical waste I'd read about stored in lots and buried in the neighborhood. I could feel it swirling down below, bubbling up to the surface. Why was I living here? Rent was cheap—that was the best and only explanation.

When I got back to the apartment, I made my uninteresting meal of macaroni and cheese. I'd gotten the wrong kind again: too orange and much too smooth a consistency. It was still early so I lay in bed and tried to read one of the books I'd started. I had five or six by my bed then. I would try one and then another, not getting very far with any of them, until it seemed like a substantial amount of time had gone by and I could turn off the light and sleep.

I didn't see him the next day, but then that wasn't unusual—days could actually go by before we bumped into one another. But I remember sort of looking for him. I thought, since he'd ask me to postpone my invitation and I hadn't approached him again, that he might approach me—for a walk, or a beer, whatever.

I began to notice that he wasn't coming or going from his apartment. It wasn't as if I was sitting at my window watching. I had a job to go to after all, for a few hours in the morning—at the time I was working for this woman who made cards and stationery; she had her own little company. So maybe he came and went while I was away; I couldn't have known, though his door and mailbox slot looked suspiciously like they hadn't been opened and the dust on our hallway floor looked exactly the same as before (only more so). I might have even sprinkled a little dirt on the floor outside our apartments, just to see if he'd been through—I'd know if there was an imprint. But for a long time nothing seemed changed.

One day I decided I ought to do something about it; or rather, one day I found myself investigating, without thinking: I was suddenly trying the knob on his door. It turned easily, and with a push, the door was open. I should have said "Hello!"—after all, I was trying to find him; it would have been proper. I didn't though. I stepped in quietly, surreptitiously. There was the smell I hadn't thought about but had associated with his apartment: a little like overcooked broccoli. There was the table we'd sat at, the low stools, the stove. I peeked around to see into the other room. I saw his mattress. The bathroom was off to the right, just as in my room (though in mine it was to the left), and I looked to see if he was there, though I knew he wasn't. And then, maybe to think things over, to study his room—I sat down on the edge of his mattress. He had a sort of desk against the wall opposite, a door really, turned on its side to make a desk for him. Without thinking about it (I was tired I guess), I lay back on the mattress. I was careful about my shoes; I didn't want to dirty it. The sheets smelled pleasant, they were real cotton ones I could tell, worn from hundreds of washings, and though the last wash had probably been some time ago, I liked the way they smelled. We had always used real cotton sheets at home and they smelled so fresh; I nudged myself into a corner and buried my face in them.

I woke in the dark in a room like mine, only backwards. He was lying next to me, naked (I could see his clothes in a heap on the floor), his face buried in the pillow. Had he seen me? It was possible he hadn't turned on the light; wouldn't I have woken if he had? I lay beside him, feeling trapped and uncertain. His skin was too white, even in the dark. I sort of lay my arm next to him, just to see what his skin felt like. And then because I couldn't really tell, I moved closer to him. He felt warm against me. In a way I wished I were naked. He shifted a little in his sleep. I touched him again, this time on the bottom of the ear, where his ear lobe was; it was soft, like a baby's skin. I had the urge to kiss it. I brought my lips close; I don't remember if I actually did it. I got up out of bed then. Quietly, very quietly, I tiptoed out of his apartment.

Not much longer after that he moved. I hadn't asked him to walk again, and he hadn't offered a beer. But once we caught each other in the hallway, like before, standing awkwardly in our doorways, and my cat rubbed up first against my legs and then against his, and I asked how he was and he answered.

Honda
a novella

I. PETUNIA & THE MR.

There was no reason to follow him, nothing remark-able about him, after all: a canvas jacket (hunting style, but I don't believe he was a hunter), jeans, worn leather shoes. A serious face, some grey in his hair. I think it was his dog, so obviously well-cared for, a black lab (chocolate labrador?) which made my feet fall behind theirs. Did he notice I was following them? Once he turned around. I smiled. He turned back but I caught up with him.

"I like your dog," I said. "May I pat him?"

He couldn't refuse me. The dog didn't mind my strok-ing; he seemed quite happy.

"What's his name?" I asked.

"It's a she ... Petunia," he said, with a note of apol-ogy, I thought, as if to say: I know it's a stupid name, but.... "Do you have a dog?" he asked.

I shook my head. "But I'm thinking of getting one...."
I knew that dog owners formed a sort of club; they all met
in the park and talked, sitting on park benches, while the
dogs ran around with their noses in the mud, dirtying up
the park with their doggy business. It was disgusting to
watch. "A dog can make life much more pleasant, don't
you think?" I asked. "Would you recommend it?"

"Absolutely," he said. He launched into the practical
matters: having enough time to walk it, cleaning up its
business, all of which was offset by the reward of constant
affection. Petunia was bored by now and began sniffing
the gutter, pulling at the man's leash as her nose traced
scents unknown to us but obviously very powerful.

Right in the middle of telling me about having to
switch dog food brands, he suddenly stopped talking.
Something had occurred to him, or perhaps he noticed I
wasn't really taking notes, not even mental ones.

"Well, I must get going, it's time. Nice meeting you,"
he told me, though the only name that had been exchanged
was Petunia's. "Good luck with getting a dog," he added,
which was, of course, very thoughtful.

I waited until they had turned the corner, until Petunia had lost my scent and found someone else's, before I
fell into step behind them. I kept more of a distance than
before; I didn't want to be noticed (but hadn't I been walking in his direction all along? Why should I turn on my
heels and pretend otherwise?). I memorized the backside
of him; I could have replicated it on paper: heels worn
down on the outside, wool socks, jeans slightly frayed at
the bottom, collar turned up, hair combed, though not all
that neatly. More window shopping, more dodging pedes-
trians, nothing out of the ordinary for these two. But then
Mr. Pseudo-Hunting Jacket stopped walking. He tied
Petunia to a parking meter, told her to wait quietly, and
disappeared into a bakery.

It was really very stupid of him to have left her on
the street, alone, where anyone might have found her,
slipped her leash from the post and made off with her. It's

true that crime is low in our small town; nonetheless, one should never assume protection. After all, there were the high-school boys who sometimes went on the prowl, not usually at 3:00 p.m., but again, who could be sure? Did he believe a higher power was watching out for him and his dog?

I watched him at the counter. He had his back turned, was pointing to a muffin in the glass case, blueberry or possibly cranberry with walnuts. I patted Petunia while I freed the little noose he'd made with her leash. He wasn't thinking about her as he ordered a cappuccino, a fact that would later haunt him, I felt sure. Petunia was only too happy to be free again; she pulled me gaily along. I let her do this until I realized he was going to catch up with us if we didn't hide. I wasn't sure where to go—it's not as if I'd thought this through ahead of time—but it occurred to me that the railroad tracks made a nice line out of sight and out of town. No train came through anymore; somewhere it had been decided our town wasn't worth a train stop and the tracks had been destroyed, leaving behind a trail through a tunnel of trees. I wondered if Mr. Hunting Jacket ever walked Petunia there, or if she was always led by her nose to cappuccino and muffins. I laughed out loud, remembering how he'd presented himself as such an authority on the care and maintenance of canines.

Petunia was straining to get off the leash, the multitude of scents along the tracks was making her a little crazy. I knew enough not to let her run loose; it wasn't me she'd come running back to but Mr. Jacket. Still, she was starting to feel like a load, jerking me along behind her, making me walk faster than I like to, and then suddenly transforming herself into a pig rooting out truffles (not that I'd ever seen one, but I'd heard about it). Where was the payoff? The slobberly doggy affection? I chose a tree stump for myself and made her sit down next to me. "Sit!" I commanded, and she did. Mr. Jacket had trained her nicely.

We sat a long time like this, Petunia looking up at me every so often with a certain expectancy. "What is it you want? Whatever it is, I don't have any," I told her and went back to drawing in the dirt with a stick. "I have your dear Petunia," I found myself writing. "Will give back in exchange for…" I didn't finish the sentence because I wasn't sure what I wanted. Money was of course the logical answer, and I felt certain Mr. Cappuccino-to-Go had plenty. But somehow money didn't set my heart beating…. The day was grey and drizzly, dreary and gristly, the time of year when the only colors seem to be variations of mud brown, grey and tan. Weren't doggy companions supposed to provide color? "Hey Petunia," I tapped her haunches with my stick, lightly of course, but it was as if she were a horse who'd gotten the signal to canter. Her leash was jerked from my hand as she took off down the trail. I ran to catch up with her, cursing her all the way, because I was out of shape and no match for a Pegasus-like canine. She was heading back toward town, covering in minutes the ground we'd walked earlier. There was no hope of catching up to her.

"You retard!" I shouted after her. "So go home! See what I care!" knowing it made no difference at all to her. She was hot for her muffin man, her Psuedo-Hunter, her Worn-Down-on-the-Heel but very rich owner. I cursed them both; if it hadn't been for the pair of them, I'd be nice and cozy at home, curled up in a blanket and sleeping. I was saying this to myself, thinking out loud as I went along, when I saw him. I slid back into the shrubbery which lined the trail, crouched behind a thick bush. I don't believe he noticed.

I was witness to their reunion. Petunia sprang up on her haunches, licking his face with a pink slobbery tongue. He covered her body with kisses, hugging her so hard that at times she was lifted off the ground. Their behavior was astounding, even to me. At one point they did a little dance together, nothing I knew the steps to. "Where were you? What happened?" he kept asking, as if Miss Petunia could answer.

They sauntered off together like that, Miss Petunia jumping up every so often to lick her owner on the chin. I

wanted to tell him what had happened: how lucky he was
that I'd come upon his Petunia, how a gang of boys had
obviously stolen her and brought her to this trail. I'd managed to free her of them, with stones and threats and
screams of animal abuse, ever so fortunately, because
clearly their intentions were not very nice ones. But the
Mr. and his dog were too far away by now; I couldn't reach
them even by running wildly. And in any case, I didn't
feel like running.

II. PIE

I settled myself in a booth and immediately saw I'd left my lights on. (Once I'd left them on for a total of ten minutes and the car had trouble starting up again. Clearly I needed a new battery—but then again, there were plenty of other things I needed and who could say which was more important?). I went outside to turn them off, noticed him on my way back. His face was large, moon-like; his eyes, sullen and dark. Those little eyes seemed to accuse me as he sat, hunched down on the passenger side of the car. I didn't like him but I felt sorry for him. It was nasty of his dad—or whoever it was—to make him wait inside the car. It was dark and rainy out, probably cold inside the Chevy Cavalier where he sat while his dad chomped on porkchops and applesauce and sloshed it down with coffee (or was it beer?).

I ordered the pork roast with apples from the waitress whose caked-on makeup only highlighted her age. But you wouldn't find me endorsing only young waitresses. That was never any of my business. Besides, it was "What can I get you honey?" I didn't mind the honey-part.

Eventually I figured out who his dad was, the only one who hadn't gone out to his car yet. He sat on a bar stool, his large derriere spilling over the stool's edge. He was taking his time, eating slowly. Watching him, the word *stool* started to work on me. Why would something you sit on and something you evacuate be called the same thing? It was obscene. I looked away from him and his too large rear end, watched the passing cars and trucks on the highway instead. There were also the cars in the parking lot to stare at, their noses all turned toward me.

It bothered me how he just sat there. He didn't move around or close his eyes to sleep, he didn't get out of the car to look for his dad in the restaurant. He just sat there, his head slightly rolled back. Very unnatural. Didn't he care that his dad had abandoned him, didn't it get him angry? It was hard to tell. My pork roast arrived. It was good and greasy. Why go out to a diner and order salad? Not me. I stuck to the dinner specials and their cousins. Of course I was often disappointed. Sometimes the whole business just wasn't very tasty. Hot and filling, but disappointing finally. I doused a bite of pork in applesauce. It wasn't bad. I survived it. I noticed he had graduated to pie, pie and coffee. Why sit on a stool when your derriere is overpowering? I figured it was his one ounce of atonement. For leaving his son in the car. It couldn't have been comfortable.

The waitress came by to ask how everything was. "Fine," I said; she'd caught me with my mouth full. I motioned for her to wait while I finished chewing, "What are your pies tonight?" She smiled as she launched into her repertoire, "We have Blueberry, Apple, Pecan, and Lemon Meringue." I wondered what he was having. "Thanks, I'll think about it," I told her. "Take your time, honey."

He took me by surprise; I hadn't noticed him getting up. He was on the way to the men's room. It was again a rear view; I hadn't caught his eyes yet. I checked my window-seat view of his son: still sitting, not yet sleeping, eyes hardly blinking.

It was my chance I realized, with his father gone in the bathroom. I could open the door to the car, tell him to make a run for it; I could get in the driver's seat, get him the hell out of there; I could invite him inside to share my dinner. The last one seemed to me the best solution; I had only to ask him. What could the father do to me after all? We were all grown-ups here. Actually, the boy was maybe twelve or thirteen, or possibly older, with a childlike appearance still. With his large white face it was hard to tell. I finished chewing, wiped my face with my napkin, took a swig of coffee. I realized I was procrastinating. I wasn't eager to go outside; at the same time I felt compelled, as if I alone had been chosen to do this. It was 7:05 p.m. and everything seemed to rest on my shoulders. I made my way out of my booth. I was almost out the restaurant when I thought I heard the bathroom door opening. I hurried outside.

I rapped on the window. He stared at me, somehow blank and angry at the same time. He didn't blink; he didn't roll the window down, he didn't do anything. I went around to the driver's side. I didn't want to scare him.

"Hey, kid, don't you want to come inside? I'll buy you dinner. They've got nice pies: Lemon Meringue, Dutch Apple, Banana Creme. Banana Creme," I repeated; for some reason he looked like a banana-creme kid to me. He was staring at me. I thought he looked interested. "Want to come in?" He didn't say anything. I noticed he was twisting his fingers together. Maybe that was his way of saying he did. "Tell you what, I'll bring you some."

I closed the door quietly, made my way back into the restaurant.

"I thought we'd lost you," the waitress said. "How about that pie now, hon?" she asked as she cleared away the remnants of my dinner for one. "Sure," I told her. "I'll have Banana Creme—to go."

But Banana Creme wasn't on the list. I felt a moment of panic. Already I'd made a promise I couldn't keep. Did his father know what I'd done? He had his back to me still; he seemed large and oblivious. I settled for Lemon Meringue, then switched to Apple. Not everyone liked lemon. It was sour after all. I worried over the choice though. Wasn't apple too plain for a kid? But apple pie was all American; surely there was a reason for this….

The father was pulling on his coat; now he was making his way to the register. I looked through the window at the Chevy Cavalier. In the dark I could barely see him; it seemed he was leaning back, eyes closed, mouth open: a small o. I tried to motion to the waitress to hurry.

He was groping for his wallet. He carried nothing in his hands for his boy, no piece of pie or packet of oyster crackers. He was going to leave. The waitress brought me a white paper bag with the pie inside. I quickly calculated my bill and her tip and made for the door.

But he was there before me, opening the door in a great act of chivalry. I had no choice but to walk through it. Outside I hesitated. My plan would never work now and I didn't have an alternative.

He started to button up his coat. "Nice evening, isn't it?"

"Sure," I said, though it was dark and rainy, nothing nice about it.

"Enjoy your pie." He winked at me, or at least I thought he did.

"Hey!" I said, but he was already sliding his bulk behind the steering wheel. He hunkered himself down, found the key to the Chevy in his pocket, fed it into the ignition. The car started up with a great burst of energy. Only then did the boy open his eyes; the small o closed into a smile. He held onto his father's arm as his father backed out of the lot. Just before they pulled into traffic, I saw the father roll down his window and thrust out his arm. It must have been the middle finger that he extended.

"So take this!" I yelled, aiming the white paper bag with its pie at his back window. The bag landed in a puddle surprisingly near where I stood. For a moment it held my attention. I could picture the pie inside, soaked, losing shape by the second.

III. Honda

I liked the name. If ever I had a child I'd name him
that. I figured it was the kind of name that would protect
him. Why did I imagine a he? No reason. Just that Honda
wasn't going to fit a girl very well. Sometimes I imagined
I already had him. I'd sit at the playground with all the
young mothers and dads with their children and I'd see
Honda playing in the sandbox. He was a good boy. He
kept to himself, never bothered anyone. Of course the sand
creations he made, castles with drawbridges and so forth,
were so fantastic that the other children begged to play
with him. Or at least help him. They would pile sand for
him. For example. Or they'd be the ones to make the tiny
patterned imprints on the castle, from twigs and leaves
and so on. Honda didn't mind them helping. He would

be so intent on his project that nothing else could really interfere. It could drive you a little crazy. When I called him to dinner, when it was dark and time to leave the park, he'd still be sitting there, piling on sand and fixing bridges. He acted like he didn't hear me.

I'd leave the park in frustration. It's easy to get mad when no one pays attention to you. It happened on one such day. I was thinking about the mothers and their spanking-clean children, the little snacks they always carried for them. Seemed like they always thought of everything. How they fell into easy conversation with one another. About their children of course. I got into my car, started up the engine. I noticed as I pulled out of the lot that the car had a different smell, a cigar smoke smell. I looked around as I drove. I could see work gloves on the passenger seat and some motorcycle magazines on the floor. None of these were things I kept in my car—so how did they get there? And the key chain—a tiny soccer ball of imitation leather—wasn't what I carried. I had a little red pocket knife, the kind with miniature scissors on it. The more I looked around the more I saw that this wasn't my car. It was blue, it was a 1982 Honda, but it was someone else's.

Of course I should have driven right back to the lot, parked the car and gotten in my own. Isn't that what you do when you realize you've gone home with someone else's raincoat? The sort of thing that happens a lot—at tea parties or restaurants. I kept on driving. I had some sort of block against turning around. Maybe because of how Honda ignored me in the park; I didn't want to be seen by all those young mothers again. Or maybe it was just inertia. Whatever it was, my foot was on the gas pedal, the gas gauge was at half-full and I was going straight ahead. Apart from the cigar smell, which was kind of homey when you got used to it, the car was actually cleaner than my own. I mean I did have a lot of junk and things in mine: dinners that were half-eaten, crumbled cookies, my broken umbrella and favorite green sweater and things. I noticed also that his upholstery wasn't torn like mine was. I really don't know how he kept it so neat. After all, it was a very old model. He actually had a blanket on the back seat to keep it cleaner. I checked it out through the rearview mirror. I thought I could see dog hair on it. So he had a dog. A doggy type of individual.

Where do you go in a car that isn't yours? It wasn't at all clear to me. So I kept on driving. It occurred to me that I could bring his car home for him. That would be a real favor since he was probably wondering where it had gone off to. I had only to find his address. I waited for a red light to pull out his registration. There it was: Michael Todd. Chestnut Hill Road. Such a pretty name for a road. I had never been there. It gave me a destination. I wasn't exactly sure how to find Chestnut Hill. I searched the side pockets for maps. I found maps of Canada and New Mexico but no local ones. Obviously this guy knew his way around. You had to give him credit for that. Or maybe it was his dog, with the nose of a pointer. Always pointing toward home. Or was that a weather vane? I wasn't sure. I had never been very good at directions. In fact, I was getting more and more lost by the second. At least I had gas. Half a tank could go pretty far. I didn't have money to buy more. If I ran out of gas, Mr. Todd was just going to have to find his car by the side of the road somewhere. A sad thought for the Mr. and his dog. But they were used to walking. That's what doggy-types did: walk all over the place. Come to think of it, he might not even miss his car, being so used to walking everywhere.

It was very pleasant this time of year: early summer. The lilacs were starting to blossom. I rolled down the window some to get a whiff of them, to kind of trade cigar smell for lilacs. They were wholesome. The road was a pretty one. I passed old barns and neatly kept houses. It was the time of year you could see people out in their gardens. All winter long you never see anyone and then suddenly they're everywhere like ants out of their tunnels: digging and planting and mowing. A lot of work surely.

But then, you get that nice flower smell. And lots of it. Or you get a clean piece of lettuce. Or a bright red radish. The possibilities are endless. Too bad I never took up gardening. With Honda there just wasn't time for it. It was one or the other. Maybe Mr. Todd had time though. In between motorcycles and dog walking, soccer and cigar smoking.

Chestnut Hill. The thing to do was to ask someone. One of those gardeners. I chose a lady with a wide brim. Her hair was white and her skin aged from the sun. Didn't she take a break in the winter? "Can you tell me how to get to Chestnut Hill?" I practiced my most polite on her.

She squinted at me. "Let me see now…. Go back to town, take the first right after the light, go up a hill, you'll see a sign for it, off to the left somewhere…."

I nodded like I knew exactly what she was talking about. Her eyes were very blue. Everything else seemed faded. I thanked her. "Your garden is beautiful," I told her. She seemed genuinely pleased. "I'd keep a garden if it weren't for my child," I added, "you get so busy, you know?"

She nodded. "My children are all grown. I probably have more time than I know what to do with. But I enjoy it really…."

I felt she was on the verge of telling me things she might regret later. "Bye ma'am, and thank you…."

Driving on a road you've already driven on isn't so much fun. Back to town. I had a bad feeling about it. I really should have kept going, looked at more and more pretty houses and hillsides, maybe even lakes and ponds. I don't know why I didn't just turn around. It was the fact that I'd been given direction, been told where to go. It was silly though, because why should I care about the Mr. and his dog? Why should I bother to return the Honda when it suited me very well, fit like a glove to my needs and personality? The faded blue upholstery, the slate blue dashboard, the gas gauge on its just-below half mark, all felt very intimate, like the Honda and I had been designed for each other. I was snug inside. I tried the radio, but quickly turned it off; I didn't like the intrusion of loud radio voices. I wanted the hum of the engine: just Honda and me, taking our time.

I noticed him as I pulled into town. He was right behind me. I sometimes see them where they're not; I see bars on a car roof—ski racks and so forth—and immediately I slow down. I don't like to take chances. But there was no mistaking this one: a spanking-white car with blue stripes and block letters: State Police. I felt confused. Should I continue straight or try to find that turn-off, the way to Chestnut Hill? My plan, which had never been a very clear one, was completely muddled now. I put on my turn signal. I was following the directions Mrs. Cornflower had given me; I was on my way, my best foot forward.

That's when the lights started flashing red to the accompaniment of high-pitched screeling. It was my worst migraine turned inside out, the flashing and screeching closing in on me, blood-shot eyes all around me. I was sweating profusely. There was nothing to do but pull over. I suppose there was the other option of a high-speed car chase, but no, I didn't feel like I had that option. I really didn't. I turned the engine off. I looked at myself in the mirror, straightened my hair. Was that Mr. Todd in the car with his dog? I thought it must be. I sat back in the Honda and waited. I felt calmer suddenly.

IV. The Way to Chestnut Hill

There is no need to discuss humiliation. The kind of interrogation the police can put you through. Accusing you of stealing someone else's car when it was an innocent mistake: the car was exactly the same as my own. And let's not forget that the owner had left his keys in it. Mr. Todd. But I'm not supposed to know his name. We were never introduced. Not by the policeman or by our own selves. It doesn't matter. I was already aware of him. Mr. Todd and his chocolate labrador. Mr. Neat and Tidy with a dog who sheds hair faster than you can vacuum. It was an innocent mistake. Even the policeman had to come around to this. After all: there was my own car looking very similar, except for the rusty grooves and pockets, in the parking lot. (Once I'd found a mouse living in a rusted-out hole, practically under the car. She'd made a little nest in there. Maybe she was pregnant and had some hairless pink babes to deliver. But after she saw me, she disappeared. I wasn't going to disturb her.)

It was a mistake. I knew enough to apologize profusely. How could I be so stupid? I even said this. More than once. I was obviously distracted. I was thinking about my son. I needed to get to the hospital to visit him. A congenital defect … (did I have to specify what it was? It seemed not). They nodded in sympathy, eventually.

Of course my own car was not driving so nicely. It was louder than his (the muffler) and the gas gauge was only a hair above empty, as it always was. This was not a fault of the car of course, but of my own economic situation. Times were tough. It's not that I didn't have a job—I did—but let me just say, the pay and hours were slight. In the past I'd had jobs which called for creativity, originality even, like when I worked for the Card Lady. I did all sorts of wonderful things for her, down to helping her with the text and the punchlines. But some things aren't meant to continue. Her company got bigger; she moved. I sometimes wondered why she didn't offer to take me with her. A sort of relocation/transfer. I wouldn't have minded. She didn't ask me though. She had her own reasons, I'm sure.

It bothered me that now my car was known. It made me suspicious as I drove through town. Word was already circulating, I felt sure. The way people looked at me as they walked, or stopped pushing their baby carriages to stare, made me uneasy. I felt sure I had a record now, at least a verbal one, at the police station. It all seemed so unfair. It could make a person very angry really. I decided not to dwell on it.

But Chestnut Hill. There was really no way I could go through life without knowing where it was. The way to Chestnut Hill…. It felt like a good song or the title of a novel. Let's just say though, driving your own car isn't the same thrill. The landscape I'd marveled at earlier didn't look so special now. Because what did I care about neatly trimmed gardens and houses? Yet minutes ago they had looked precious, inviting even. Sometimes I just couldn't maintain my positive energy. I'd read those books on positive thinking; I'd put in my time in that arena. Sure ... whatever makes you happy. The truth is, sometimes you just want to let loose some zoo animals to tromp on the petunias and munch on the roses. Besides, an elephant or hippopotamus could liven things up. You get bored looking at all that greenery. A hunk of grey isn't such a bad thing after all—I felt better just thinking about it.

I had every intention of going to Chestnut Hill. Who knows? Maybe the view from up there would be something to behold. Would make everything else worth it. But the whole idea started sitting heavy with me, like half-cooked bread in my stomach. The experience of being pulled over by the police, no matter how much I thought about baby mice and hippopotamuses, left me feeling sour. There was no way around it. I even tried to get my mind settled on Honda; he could usually cheer me up, with his dark hair and eyes, his intense child-like seriousness. But I'd put him in the hospital with a congenital defect. This also bothered me. That I'd resorted to such an extreme. Obviously I'd felt desperate. It would take time for me to recover my equilibrium. Driving wasn't going to do it.

I pulled off by the side of the road, parked my car, and started walking. It was late afternoon, almost evening. The thing is, in the summertime the days are so long you never know what to do with them. They stretch out before you, the sun still shining bright past five, six, seven in the evening. What do people do with so much sunniness? There were times I just wanted to crawl into bed, into a nice dark cave of stillness. Maybe that's why I found myself entering the woods.

Even the woods turn green in the summertime. It's the most amazing thing. This absolute push toward greenery. Never mind that it's a prickerbush, skunk cabbage or poison ivy, it's still green and shiny. I always wear long pants; I'm not going to risk any of those bushes or leaves touching me. I don't trust any of it. Like fiddleheads, those ferny things. I've heard people eat them. For breakfast. Imagine! Fry them up and serve them in restaurants. Someone told me about it. Or else I overheard it: "I'm just dying to eat those fiddleheads! I can't wait til they're in season." Imagine that: fiddlehead season. You'd think they were discussing violins. The truth is, everything has gotten mixed-up. People eat things for breakfast now I don't even know the names of. Astonishing things.

I sat down at the base of a tree. I leaned into it. It felt friendly. Maybe I could even fall asleep here, wake up to a forest-floor breakfast. The idea was intriguing. I closed my eyes. I felt the sun disappear.

V. Mrs. Barlow

I wanted to let things blow over. So I lay low for a while. Sure, I went to work. I folded my stack of flyers very professionally. But I didn't talk to anyone. I had nothing to say. I had a bad feeling about my car still, so I took long walks instead. I found roads to walk on I'd never seen before. I often got tired. I'd take a breather, parking myself in a patch of grass, lying back to catch the breeze blowing through. Things were blowing over—I could feel it.

I watched a lady check her mailbox three times before the mailman came. Didn't she know the mailman only comes once and never on Sunday? She was waiting for something wonderful. What could it be? I felt excited for her. It was a nice fat check or it was a gift or it was a love letter. But love letters are hardly written anymore. People rely on the phone now. I don't have a phone. As a result, I'll never get a love call. Or a wrong number. I would enjoy that once in a while: "Is Melanie there?" "WHO? Mr., you have the wrong number...." That's the loss I settled for when I didn't buy into the phone company. But then, you can't have everything. Life is like that. A series of compromises.

I watched a plane fly overhead. People going places. Places important. Once in a while a car rumbled by, throwing dust in my face. I was bored but I didn't want to admit that. I was waiting, waiting for something wonderful, just like Mrs. Postbox. We had something in common after all. If only she'd invite me in for tea. We could talk about it then: all those wonderful things. But I knew I'd be a fright to her. With dust on my pantslegs and rhinoceros elbow. Once when I was a child I fell into a prickerbush; my arm got scratched and when I looked at it, really examined it, I saw that the skin on my elbow was loose and wrinkly—frighteningly ugly, in a way I'd never seen before. I complained to my mother. "Rhinoceros elbow," was what she told me. I realized then that there was a small rhinoceros hiding in the prickerbush. I steered clear of the bush after that; I didn't want him infecting me again.

But what was Mrs. Postbox up to? A robust lady with white hair, she reminded me of my grade-school teacher. It might have been her, except that Mrs. Barlow had died some time ago. Still, it is my philosophy that there is a finite number of individuals. If you look at people, really study faces, you begin to see how similar everyone looks to each other.

I remember when I was first visited by this revelation. About three years ago I was sitting in this diner. And the more I sat there, drinking coffee and watching the other customers, the more I saw that everyone in the diner, every single person, reminded me of someone I'd seen before. I would have sworn I'd actually already met every single one of them, except this was in a town I'd never been to before, and that kind of thinking isn't logical. There was even a woman who looked like me. When I looked at her, I saw that I was staring at myself. It was unnerving. I went into the bathroom to check myself in the mirror, just to see that I wasn't her. Of course I did find differences—her hair was cut shorter and was dyed, I think, a mahogany tinge to it—but the shape of our faces and the color of our eyes were much too similar. The interesting thing was that she was smoking. She was smoking and smoking, lighting one cigarette after another, as she sat talking to her companion (a skinny man, with a face that was too long for him). I myself had never smoked. But seeing her smoking like that, I saw how someone else who was like me would do something like that. It made me want to try it. Finally, I couldn't stop myself. I went right up to her table.

"Excuse me," I said, "could you lend me a cigarette?"

"I won't lend you one, because I don't want it back, but here, you can have one."

She and her companion laughed. They laughed too much for my comfort. I had wanted to see her face when she looked at me—what would she do when she saw it was her own self she was looking at? But she kept her eyes on her friend; she might as well have been hypnotized. She was trying hard to avoid it—the shock of recognition, which is what I call it.

But what was Mrs. Postbox doing? I suddenly needed a cigarette very badly. I had only to ask. Asking never hurt anyone. At worst it was: "*WHO*? You have the wrong number…." And how could you be held responsible for dialing a wrong number? It was just a mistake, a mechanism in the phone that decided every so often to dial incorrectly. Life holds a certain number of mistakes for each of us. I hadn't reached my quota yet.

I knocked on her door. She took a long time coming. Strange, I thought, since there was only one floor. Maybe she was napping. If so, I could understand the impulse.

She opened the door slowly. "I'm simply not interested. My choice in religion was squared away years ago

and I have neither the money nor the inclination to purchase…"

"Oh no, I'm not selling anything. I just wanted to ask
a favor."

"Well, what is it then?"

Her attitude threw me. She wasn't at all like Mrs.
Barlow. Mrs. Barlow was much more lady-like, really very
generous. "I wondered if I could use your phone…?"

"Well, I suppose … is it your car? Did something happen?"

I nodded. "It came to a stop … it won't start up again."

"I suppose you need a jump? But I haven't any jumper
cables, and I wouldn't know how to use them if I did…."

"No, please, just your phone…."

She was making me nervous. Her hawklike presence
was very exasperating.

"Well, here it is then." She directed me to a phone sitting on a small table in the living room. It was placed very
neatly on a lace cloth, like it was another piece of decora-
tion, a china figurine or something. She probably even
dusted it. This was the sort of house where if the chinaman
selling balloons was moved a hair closer to the duck with
the parasol, Mrs. Postbox would notice. She would lie awake
at night wondering how it'd happened. I had to stop this
line of thinking and concentrate on dialing.

"Is it a local call?"

"Oh yes, right here in town." A man's voice answered.
"Hello? Is Bob there?"

"You mean Rob?"

"Sure," I said.

"Hey Rob!!!" I heard, then silence, then, "Hello. Rob
speaking."

"Hi Rob, look I'm in a jam. My car won't start, I need
a jump."

"But where are you? Do I know you?"

"Sort of," I told him. "I'll explain when you get here."
I gave him a location—the corner of Wylie and Irving (a
place I hadn't been to recently and didn't want to revisit),

thanked him, then thanked Mrs. Postbox with her house as tidy as a postage stamp.

"You have such a darling home," I told her. "And such a cute mailbox. You must get lots of nice mail and things. I wish I did. I live in an apartment which is not the same as a rural route, not the same at all. But I'm sure you know that…." She was staring at me. Something I'd said had unsettled her. "Well, I better get to my car now. Thanks again! Thanks a million! By the way," I was determined to go ahead with it, "you wouldn't have a cigarette, would you?"

"You're asking me to help you poison yourself?"

"If you want to look at it like that…"

"Well, if you don't have a problem with that, then I can assure you I don't either." She opened a drawer jammed full of scrambled items (so that was where anything that looked out of place went), fished out a package of Kents. I didn't know they made them anymore. She opened the pack. "Help yourself."

"Just one will do." I slid one out. "Thank you, Mrs. —. Thank you so much. I'm off now." She nodded, almost smiled I thought. And the more I looked at her, the more I saw that she really was Mrs. Barlow. People have a funny way of representing themselves to you.

The Kent was quite stale. I realized I was probably smoking a cigarette of 1972 vintage, left behind when Mrs. Barlow quit smoking. It made me vaguely nauseous. What was she doing, lying in wait with her twenty-year-old cigarette pack for some unsuspecting visitor? Poison indeed. Nonetheless I kept smoking.

It had suddenly gotten very gusty. It was best to get home. After all, I'd left Honda there all alone.

In bed I got comfortable with my favorite book: *The Random House Dictionary*, paperback edition. On the back I noticed something I hadn't seen before: "…prepared by its permanent lexicographic staff…." I felt they were boasting.

Perhaps other dictionaries had no permanent staff, but only hundreds of freelancers. Then again, it did seem like something worth boasting about. It was really a dream job: imagine being paid to find all those words, and the phrases to define them, and to know that you were permanently employed. I opened it up at random (I took my cue from the title) as I always did and found my word: *shunpike*, to avoid turnpikes or expressways to travel more leisurely and to avoid tolls.

Shunpike. I felt it defined my life entirely. Avoiding turnpikes, escaping tolls, travelling more leisurely. Somehow the dictionary always gave me purpose. I looked up *shun* (to avoid habitually) and *pike* (a slender freshwater fish having a long, flat snout), and found *piker*: a person who does something in a contemptibly small or cheap way.

What a piker. It was a good word. One I could feel satisfied with, one I could close the book to.

I felt successful. I was not on the permanent staff, but on the other hand, I'd avoided tolls and travelled leisurely. And though there were surely millions of pikers in the world, I knew I was not among them.

VI. THE RATE OF CRIME

It's funny how you can go along always buying the same kind and then suddenly it isn't at all appetizing, seems all wrong in fact. There were so many to choose from and yet so few really good ones. Finally I settled for one (settled is the right word, I wasn't enthusiastic about it, it was in no way perfect): a Milky Way. I laid it on the counter, counted out my change, then pushed my two quarters and three pennies toward the lady who smiled too long at me.

It wasn't worth that kind of smiling. She seemed to know it was my lunch, and disapproved, as so many others do, of candy bars for lunch. So that the smile was a kind of smirkiness. And for an old lady. I was surprised. "Old piker," I almost said to her, then changed my mind.

"Did you know," I spoke casually, "that chocolate can ward off appendicitis? "

"Really, I never…"

"Yes, yes, you didn't read that the other day? A little chocolate every day can protect you from ever having to get your vermiform appendix removed."

"Well, I never … the things you read about … I never would have guessed…."

There were at least six different newspapers on sale behind her. There was really no excuse for being so uninformed. But why badger her about it? She was old, probably had lots to think about: hundreds of grandchildren, a long life with a man who talked in his sleep and spoke with his mouth full. Besides, it bothered me that I'd opened up to her, gone off on such an inconsequential tangent. Because now, each and every time I set foot in her store, I'd have to say something to her. It's better not to get started with people behind counters. Once you do, there's no turning back; they expect you to just go further, reveal more and more, enlarging and enlarging on your small talking. And the thing of it is, in a small town you just don't have a lot of options. I'd opened my mouth to the Pharmacy Lady; just how many places were left where I hadn't talked to anyone, where I could go in, choose and pay for a candy bar without having to make commentary? My choices were all too quickly diminishing. It made it very hard to enjoy my Milky Way.

I made the attempt nonetheless. I sat in my car and pulled the wrapper off. The chocolate stuck to my fingers. It was a sticky summer day, the kind of weather you wish God had not invented. Who was it for? Salamanders maybe, but not people. Could it be true we descended from fish? I'd read that somewhere, just the other day, how our ears used to be gills. How the fluid in our ears was directly linked to fish hearing underwater. Like the lady said, "the things you read about…"

The candy bar made me feel vaguely sick. It usually did. The perfect chocolate bar had yet to be invented. On the other hand, air conditioning might have made all the difference. Both my car and my apartment lacked this attractive feature. The heat was creeping up from the asphalt. You could almost see it: rising in waves. It was days like this I imagined myself living at the edge of the ocean. I had a little beach house and every day I'd wander down to the sea. Of course Honda was with me. The two of us would make our way down with our picnic basket, bathing suits, and toy boats. The sun was hot but the water was invigorating. Honda was so remarkable; with very little help from me he'd taught himself to swim. Of course this meant he swam out farther than he should have and I was constantly telling him to be careful. I didn't want any lobsters taking nips at him.

It was very peaceful. I wanted to linger there, but the fact remained: the car was sweltering. I could easily die in it—and how long before someone found me, parked in the middle of our little shopping center, my body swollen and bloated? My apartment was also an overheated cell. The kind of place to sit and write your last thoughts in. The ones that crawl through, at the same pace as the spider which makes its way across your notebook. Thinking it isn't being noticed, that your room is an entire world, free for the exploring. So that your last thoughts consist of nothing more than the rate of a spider crawling across a page. And then you shut your notebook on him. Just a smudge caught between the pages.

Someone once said that the rate of crime is directly linked to temperature—in intense heat waves crime soars. Which must mean that in the coldest regions—Antarctica, maybe—there is no crime to speak of.

I started up my car. It was time to leave behind this strip of asphalt. I had things to do, places to go. I drove fast, to catch more of the hot air blowing through my window. I remembered a back road I'd been on once, winding through a tunnel of trees. It might be cooler there; at least the greenery would be something to rest my eyes on.

I did a lot of driving to find that road, a lot of driving with the gas gauge dangerously close to empty. It bothered me that when I found it, another car was coming right behind me. Maybe I should have pulled over to let it pass. Instead I kept on driving. It could pass me if it wanted to, I kept thinking. But it didn't pass me; it kept right on my tail. A flock of crows was settling under the trees by the side of the road, and then this strange thing happened: one of the crows flew directly in front of me. He was huge and black, flying too low, just the height of my car hood. I went to brake but somehow my foot landed on the accelerator instead. I hit that crow hard, right in its belly, and watched it bounce off my hood. It fell to the side of the road.

I felt hot and cold. I wanted to stop and do something—if it was dead, maybe I should bury it—but that white car was right behind me, making me nervous and sweaty, unable to decide about anything. That car was probably the reason I'd killed the crow in the first place. It seemed like a bad omen and five miles or so later, I did pull off the road. I was shaking, just a little. Of course it was not the first animal I'd ever killed. My list was no shorter or longer than anyone else's. If people were really honest, you'd see how many animals they killed every day. After all, how many fresh small carcasses do we see as we drive quietly along? An awful lot of them. Much more than any one person would like to admit to. I opened the glove compartment and took out the list I'd started some time ago: 1 snake, 3 chipmunks, 1 snapping turtle, 2 frogs. I added: 1 large black crow.

VII. Idle Hour

Now, what did it mean to "eat crow"? I wasn't going to eat any of it. But I suddenly felt I'd gotten off the shunpike. I had the urge to drive back the five miles or so to find the bird. Just to see the state I'd left him in. How was I going to explain this to Honda? "Your mother killed a large black bird, for no reason, but that a car was nipping at her heels like a white terrier...." It was true then, what that "friend" had said some years ago, when I wanted to keep a stray cat we'd found and he wouldn't let me: "You wouldn't make a good mother." In short, that remark ended our "friendship." "You wouldn't make a good mother...." What did he have, a barometer for checking out people's mothering instincts? And mine, according to him, didn't even register. Well, things were very different

now—Honda could attest to that. I was completely devoted. True, I sometimes forgot to put his socks on, or
didn't wash his hair as often as I should have, but anyone
could see how devoted I was, how my very existence de-
pended on him. "I couldn't live without him...." Isn't that
what mothers said? Well, it was true for me as well.

I realized I'd driven back, retraced my steps, so to
speak—my tire tracks—without having found the crow.
There were three explanations, it seemed to me, any one
of which might be possible: I'd driven by without seeing
him; I hadn't reached him; or I hadn't actually killed him
(though I *had* seen him thud onto the roadside). I kept on
driving. The little red dot to show "scraping bottom of the
gas barrel" flickered on and off, and soon my car was sput-
tering, apparently on its last drops of gas. Whatever had
made me go back and look for it? I'd gotten myself into a
quandary now, a pickle, a real quagmire.... Oh the thick
mud of it! I pulled off to the side of the road, turned off
the ignition, and rested my head on the wheel, a picture
of utter dejection.

A car pulled up beside me.

"Are you okay? Can I help with anything?"

The lady of the voice had dark hair and eyes; there
was something arresting about her. "I'm out of gas...." I
managed to tell her.

She offered to drive me to the nearest gas station "no
more than ten miles from here," was what she said.

I locked my car. How sad it looked by the side of the
road. It was such a good car too ... it was remiss of me to
leave it alone so often.

I noticed that the lady's thick hair was turning grey,
gradually. And her skin was nicely tan. I remembered a
teacher I'd had, long after Mrs. Barlow.... It came back to
me, how I would find myself staring at her (but what else
were you supposed to do with a teacher who stood in front
of you every day?). She was looking right at me when she
spoke to the class about annoying phone rings and dogs
who wouldn't stop barking at 3 a.m....

"My name is Vicky," this one was saying. (Yes, that was the name of my teacher, wasn't it?) "And you are...?"

"Listen, Miss —, did you happen, when you were driving along, to spot a dead crow by the side of the road?"

She stared at me. "No.... It would be strange to see crows on this wooded road. They prefer the wide open spaces, cornfields and such..."

"The wide open spaces ... is that true?" I hunched in my seat. "So, it would be unusual for a flock of them, or even one, to be on this road, and if one got hit, one could say it was its own fault...."

"Well, I wouldn't go that far," Miss Vicky told me. "They're beautiful birds, it's just that no one pays attention to them. They're considered common, the common crow.... But I've always thought they were sort of regal, you know?"

She smiled at me. How odd, I thought. Very odd that Miss Vicky should appear after all these years on this road. ("I've changed my phone number. I've disconnected my phone," she told us one morning, her dark eyes singling me out as she spoke. But why should she bother to tell me about her private life? Her telephone apparatus?)

The tree branches swooped down low and Miss Vicky's Saab was brushed by their feathery arms. She was humming to herself as I watched a strand of hair which had fallen loose from the others, settle itself on her shoulder. She wore a black vest, buttoned-up (nothing underneath), and black jeans. Why wear black in the heat of summer? She was different that way.

"I used to drive this road every day," she stopped humming to tell me. "Isn't it beautiful? Do you know that road that branches off of it? Idle Hour Road, it's called. I used to pass by it and I never had an idle hour to drive down it, but I would wonder ... and then one day I purposely drove to find it, so I could see what it led to and do you know that road was so idle, so overgrown with grass and weeds and small shrubbery that it was impossible to drive down? So that you'd need more like an idle week to get down that thing!" She laughed like she'd made an enormous joke.

Whatever was she going on about? Miss V. was as crazy as ever, more so now that she had grey in her hair. "You know, Miss … I think I'll get out here. I can walk the rest…"

"But why? We're almost there. Is it that you love to walk?"

She looked at me and her dark eyes were again just like my teacher's. (She'd given me a D-. Who ever heard of getting a D-?) "We're almost there," she said again. "Would you like me to drive you back to your car? Otherwise, you'll have to walk with the gas. It won't be any trouble for me."

What did she do? Spend her time driving around, picking up strays and dropping them off places? A real-live Good Samaritan. "Don't you have to go to work, Miss —?"

"I do, but I'm off for the summer. Fortunately. And please don't call me Miss—my name is Vicky."

She'd brought in that article for me to read, made an appointment with that counselor. (How do you spend your evenings? Do you have any friends? What is your social life like then? Tell me about your daydreams.) "Do you have a dog?" I asked her, just to make conversation.

"Why yes, how did you know? Charlie, a basset hound."

"Isn't that great?" I said, without enthusiasm.

"And you? Do you have pets?"

"No, not with a child. I'm much too busy for pets or a garden…."

"Where is your child now?"

I looked at her. It was again a trick question, just like Miss V. in class, when she knew the answer and went ahead and asked you anyway.

"He's with his father." A lie. Honda did not have a father—I'd never given him one.

"Well, here we are." We had pulled into a rinky-dink station, more like a general store with a gas pump. There were various problems. I only had three dollars in my pocket.

"Will you take a ride back? I do have an idle hour," she laughed. Her pet joke again. I paid for three dollars of gas, filling some empty milk jugs Miss V. had conveniently provided me with.

"Tell me," she said, once I'd reseated myself, "Why were you out on this road? Just now—?"

What could I say? That I lacked air conditioning? "I got a little lost. I got off track," I said. We were driving back through the tunnel of trees. There was a dark pit in my stomach, a hollowed out feeling, like when I hadn't eaten for too many hours: a scooped out melon of a stomach, too close to the rind. (What do you do when you can't sleep? Do you ever go for walks? Are you familiar with the neighborhood of North Pierpont?)

Miss V. had fallen strangely silent. It wasn't like her not to talk. She began to hum, a different tune from before, but only faintly. I remembered to look for the crow. I was going to have to cross him off my list; it was wrong, after all, to include 1 Black Crow when he had managed to sit up and cart himself off very nicely.

We said our goodbyes. I thanked her; I did it more than once, maybe four times altogether. She would expect that. "Take care of yourself now," she said. "Sure," I answered.

Pouring the gasoline into my tank without spilling most of it was some work. I finished and for some minutes I just sat in my car. My hands held the wheel and I saw that my fingers were trembling. Was it the difficult maneuver of the gasoline or being pursued by Miss V.? After so many years, how had she found me? She'd come back somehow, a black crow of a woman, a giant mocking bird; she'd come back to taunt me.

I suddenly wanted my own bed very badly. I drove quickly, too fast, though careful not to hit any stray furry or feathered creatures. Out of the corner of my eye I saw some white block letters on a metal sign: Idle Hour Road. My heart beat fast as I drove past.

VIII. Positive Thinking

There were some people I needed to avoid. My land-lord, for instance. (When did he get such a lofty name in life? Just think: own a building and you get to be a noble-man or something.) I needed to steer clear for the obvious reasons: I had neglected to pay my rent. Well, we weren't too far into the month so no crime had been committed. In fact, he really couldn't complain yet. The check was in the mail or it was on its way to his mailbox, hand-delivered, or it had fallen into a puddle and was drying off in my room. Of course, what could be duller than waiting for a check to dry? I had to get out of my apartment, get my legs walking. Of course I would have preferred driving, but my financial state was a little precarious. I'd already rounded up all the change—pennies mostly—I could find in my apartment, packed the little paper cylinders. At the bank I got some crisp green bills in exchange, so light in weight I knew they would never be enough to pay the rent with.

It was better not to think about such things. Thinking never got you anywhere. Far better to be a person of action. Life was not about waiting around for Miss V. to show up and rescue you. Besides, there were things I had to get, things Honda needed for the start of school—crayons and pencils and so forth—as if I didn't already have enough to consider. On the other hand, sometimes kids left these things behind at the playground; once I found a whole set of markers resting on a bench with all the colors of the rainbow, from purple to lime-green, taped neatly shut in a box. Clearly a teacher had forgotten them. At the time I didn't take them, but later I realized I should have. Because someone else would surely, and why shouldn't it be me, a person of action? Why shouldn't Honda have the very best in life, down to the teacher's editions?

I walked as far as my car. I had calculated my finances: I could pay for a few dollars worth of gas and still have some left over for a Milky Way and a pack of Marlboros. The air was crisp and clear—it was that time of year when people like to watch the leaves change color as they drop down beside you. I like it too, I won't pretend I don't—but I can't help remembering what comes next: grey dreary drizzle and such ice-block coldness ... but why be so pessimistic? I'd forgotten my positive thinking lessons already. Those mantras came back to me suddenly: how we'd sat in a circle and repeated them after the leader. I can do it ... I will do it ... Nothing is too difficult.... We had to visualize ourselves climbing a mountain; one by one we got to the top of it as everyone else cheered. But were we all visualizing the same size mountain? What if my mountain was a lot smaller than everybody else's? In fact, my mountain *was* very small—just an anthill really—but nobody else seemed to notice. In any case, I had trouble concentrating; I kept thinking: how did I end up in a room with purple carpet and a pink ceiling and all of these strangers? The truth is the Card Lady had sent me. I suppose she thought I'd get inspired and it would rub off on my work for her. But you can see where it got me. She moved on without me, and what good is it then to say: I can do it, I'm climbing this mountain?

No wonder I'd forgotten to indulge in positive thinking. Come to think of it, it had all had a very poor outcome. Very poor indeed. I thought about this as I drove along. It was worth considering, it seemed to me. Because I didn't want to make that mistake again. Could it be that that sort of positive thinking, of visualization, as they called it, actually backfired? Because while you spend your time imagining delightful scenarios, circumstances are conspiring against the very picture you're creating....

It struck me as an odd coincidence that just as I was remembering about climbing mountains I was in all actuality driving up one. True, it was not a real mountain, but this was no anthill either. My Honda was struggling to get into gear. At the top I pulled over to rest a moment. The air was so quiet it sounded suspicious. Clearly this was a Monday or a Tuesday with everyone in their little work station.... I knew I should be parked in my own little station—my finances told me this—but a mother should be with her children; I didn't see why I should give that up in exchange for a couple of dollars. After all, Honda would be starting school soon and how often would I see him then?

The thought of first grade made me shudder. I'd had a terrible experience myself, softened only by Mrs. Barlow. I'd been called such a number of names, things which gave me legitimate stomach aches and hearing problems. My clothes, my shoes, even my lunch bag were suspect.... It didn't matter. I had my own world. Hocus, pocus, dominocus ... if someone was mean to me, I'd lie in bed at night imagining him (or her) with a big X on his face. The results worked very nicely. The next day the boy was invisible to me, completely insignificant—I no longer saw him. Let's not start analyzing just how this happened—these things fall apart under close scrutiny. The relevant fact is: I was worried for Honda. I decided to buy him some black charcoal pencil sticks, just in case he encountered the same kind of behavior. This led me to wonder why I would bother to send him at all—? He was, after all, so much smarter than children his age, having learned to read, to swim, to talk, so far ahead of all the other babies…. He was going to get bored; I didn't need a school psychologist to tell me that. But what would I do all day with him home? I needed to start making money…. These were the kinds of thoughts which ran through my head, typical motherhood thoughts, nothing out of the ordinary.

We took the long route home, a route which took us past the elementary school. The Crossing Guard stood beside the road as she always did, Monday through Friday, bundled up in an orange vest, waiting for her charges. And then I did something I'd never done before: I raised my hand and waved to her. She smiled and waved back.

Astonishing. How easy that had been! But what was I thinking? That was Honda's school, Honda's crossing guard…. Of course—she had recognized me. Which led me to wonder why I hadn't dropped Honda off at school today? Or let the school bus take him? I felt confused. Then I remembered … I hadn't started him there yet. Why rush things? Anyway, it was almost winter, not the start of the school year. There was time yet.

I pulled over and parked by the side of the road. Rather than turn around (and waste gas), I walked along the sidewalk the half mile or so back.

She was older than I'd imagined. She wore an orange cap with earflaps to go with her outfit. "Hello!" I said, "I was wondering…" and then it came out, what I hadn't known I would say: "Do you know if they need any more Crossing Guards at the school? Are they looking for new applicants? Or maybe, at another school?"

"Well, I really couldn't say," she told me. "Why don't you ask Mrs. Thompson? I really couldn't say myself …

maybe a back-up … someone to pick up where I leave off, I mean, fill in on a sick day…. But I'll tell you something," she was smiling, looking about to confide a secret, "the pay is terrible! You won't be able to make a living … and it's so boring … standing here all morning and afternoon, even in the winter when your toes are fucking freezing!"

I was staring at her orange earflaps. In my head I was trying her whole outfit on: the vest, the hat. It was all a little too snug, too constricting, finally.

"Is something wrong?" she asked me.

"Oh no," I told her, "I was just thinking … about my son, I've got to get back…."

"Oh," she said, and she looked confused, "You have a son—what's his name?"

"Honda," I told her.

"Honda?" She laughed. "Is that his real name?"

Of course it was. Did she have a problem? "Listen, Miss—"

"Cindy … I'm sorry, I didn't mean—"

"Listen, Miss Cindy Sorry…" Then suddenly it came back to me: that first day of school when I didn't know which bus to take … Cindy was the girl who'd misdirected me, on purpose … a long bus ride that went nowhere near where I lived….

"Look, I'm sorry. I didn't mean—"

I'd gotten off at a stranger's house, pretending it was my own—I didn't want the bus driver to know my predicament. But of course I wasn't called inside for milk and cookies. In fact, there was quite a lot of shouting coming from that particular house and so I decided to make my way back to my own. It took me the rest of the day to find it. And of course no one noticed how late I was, much later than I'd ever been…. Unbelievable that now, years later though it was, Cindy Sorry had been put in charge of youngsters. Incredible, really.

"If I were you," I told her, concentrating on the blank patch of forehead, right beneath her orange cap, "I'd start thinking about resigning. Why wait until they find out?

You're better off quitting—that way you can avoid scandal. The inevitable SCANDAL…"

"Are you nuts? What are you talking about? I'm sorry if I—"

I waved her off as I walked back. Cindy Sorry hadn't changed one iota. At least I hadn't enrolled Honda there. But what a travesty the Crossing Guard in this town was—unworthy, like so many others, of her title.

IX. P.O. Box 229

Just the other day I drove by Mrs. Barlow's and saw that her mailbox was all smashed. Now who would do a thing like that? Must have been a gang of boys acting foolish. With no respect for other people's property. I'd like to show them a thing or two. And later, when I bought the local paper, I noticed a letter:

> I'm writing to complain about the rash of vandalism occurring in our town.... Most recently my mailbox was a victim ... what is happening to the respect for others our community used to be known for?
> Signed, Rose Whitehouse

It was an interesting point. But just when did our community get this reputation for respect? It was the first I'd heard about it ... I would have liked to question her on this point over tea, but my last visit had not been entirely successful, had not really included an invitation to return ... I felt bad for her though, and thought a note to her mangled mailbox might make her feel better.

Dear Mrs. Barlow,

I understand you go by the name of Whitehouse now—did you remarry or did you take back your original name when Mr. Barlow passed away (or was it divorce?), or did you choose Whitehouse on a whim—it matches your surroundings—a way to blend in, that's true, but a little presidential, isn't it? Especially for an ex-first-grade teacher? Of course what you call yourself is none of my concern, has nothing to do with my writing you. It's about the unfortunate incident regarding your mailbox. I wonder who you hold responsible? It seems to me there are a few possibilities—I'd be pleased to discuss them with you.

Yours Truly,

M. Maddox

p.s. I hope that, when you write me, you'll sign your real name, Mrs. Barlow. I can't help preferring it. Also there's another matter I'd like to discuss with you. A former student, now employed—wrongfully. More anon.

There's something therapeutic about getting your feelings out on paper. I looked around for an envelope and stamp and noticed the check to my landlord, still not sent and without funds to back it. I felt depressed suddenly. Yet it reassured me to know I had no phone—I knew it'd be ringing now if I did, conspiring with Mr. House-Rich to wring out the rent from me. Besides, with a phone you had to worry about breakdowns, or the line going out, or death threats made (anonymously of course) by young hoodlums. I, on the other hand, had peace of mind. And since my mailbox was in the local P.O., unlike the unlucky Mrs. Barlow's, I didn't have to worry about vandalism either, unless an ex-postal worker was going to come in shooting off locks, etc. But that would be a federal crime and out of my jurisdiction. It was a shame that I'd never been called to jury duty. In fact, it bothered me quite a lot; justice was something I'd have liked to administer. Yet to this day I'd gotten no notice telling me to appear in said court at such and such location. Or did they contact you by phone? In that case, it was discrimination, pure and simple, against non-phone owners. But I wasn't going to get worked up about this. I had other worries at the moment.

Having found an envelope but no stamp, I decided to deliver the letter in person—in person to her broken mailbox, that is. It took me awhile to find her house again; we drove back roads that seemed to be going nowhere. Years and years of never wanting to backtrack had taken their toll perhaps: now I couldn't find the same route when I wanted to. Honda of course didn't like it when this happened. Unlike me, he was a very direct sort of person. He seemed convinced we were never going to find anything and started taking it out on me. He tried hard to hit me with his small fists from where he sat (he couldn't reach); he looked like he was ready to bite me.

"Honda," I told him, "that's how animals act, not children. Behave yourself…." He wasn't listening to me. Which made me angry. Did he think he was already too old to take orders? Was I really that ineffectual? Just as I was beginning to lose all patience (I might have hit him myself), we saw it: the little white house on the hillside.

There was just one small problem. There stood the post by the road at the end of her driveway, yet nothing whatsoever sat on top of it. What a strange sight. A perversion, almost. To live on a rural route in the country with no mailbox…. Where could it be? Rob slash Bob was fixing it, or else Mrs. Barlow was engaged in a form of protest by keeping it out of the picture…. And who could blame her? But I had a letter for her. And I now had the problem of how to deliver it.

For a long while we sat in the car. It's terrible when you have a plan and then quite suddenly you discover things are not as you conceived them—you sit, forced to watch everything crumble out from under you…. I felt hot with disappointment. Yet it was cold, there was snow everywhere: ugly dirty snow hardened into crusty layers. I parked my car and walked down Mrs. Barlow's driveway. No one was home. There was nothing to do but slip the envelope under her door and hope that she found it. Yes, of course she would; with her home as neat and tidy as a postage stamp, a legal-size white envelope would show up very nicely.

The next step made itself clear to me: go home and wait for her reply to arrive in P.O. Box 229. Despite the dreary ugly snow, I was almost tingling. Mrs. Barlow was not one to let me down, I felt sure of it.

X. The Season of Snowplows

I folded more than 2,000 flyers. You'd think there'd be a machine to do this sort of thing. Most likely there is, but The Valley Print Shop hadn't invested in one, and so I had a job, though a purely pathetic one. We haven't seen you in a while, Miss A. said when I came in. We left a note in your place ... didn't you get it? Yes, I did, can't you see I'm here now? Yes, but it's a day and a half later ... that's not good enough.... Why don't you get a phone? And so on and so forth; that's how the conversation went.

The flyer advertised the Annual Fireman's Ball, a benefit for the local fire station. Well, I wasn't going to go. Besides the $20 fee (for couples!), who would look after Honda? The flyers were bright red, which made sense I guess, especially since the event was set for the 14th of

February. Not that any of these dates meant anything. I'd gotten through December 25th and January 1st, for example, without ever considering what these random numbers represented. Of course one might argue that I was depriving Honda. So, go ahead and argue. It was no one's business but mine. I was tired of people butting in where they weren't wanted: too many to bother counting—even Mrs. Barlow, who hadn't replied to my letter, despite my waiting and long periods of concentration.

Don't you have any more work for me? I asked, and was told to stuff the flyers into envelopes for distribution by the Post Office. After that, I was given the supermarket flyers to insert in the local paper. The local paper. I opened it to this week's letters:

Dear Editor:
Like Mrs. Whitehouse, my mailbox was also recently crushed, almost beyond recognition. And so I sympathize with her, and yet I cannot agree with her conclusion: As we are just now experiencing the dead of winter, The Season of Snowplows, might we not also deduce that a snowplow was the cause of said destruction? In the case of my own mailbox, I know this to be the answer. And as members of our community are hard at work, morning, day and night, clearing the road for safe travel, can we blame them for mangling a few mailboxes here and there? Yes, they should take care, but bear in mind: the price of a new mailbox, U.S. Government Approved, at our local Department Store, is only $6.99, standard size. No, we should not have to buy new mailboxes when the original one, under normal conditions, can easily last 10-15 years. But again, we are in The Season of Snowplows, not normal conditions…. At the very least, let us not throw blame where it does not belong.
Respectfully yours,
V.R. Hale

The Season of Snowplows…. Why hadn't I thought of that? But with P.O. Box 229 instead of a U.S. Approved mailbox on a rural route, how could I have ever arrived at that conclusion? Still, I was stabbed with regret, remembering the letter I'd written Mrs. Barlow, a silly letter full of sympathy. Now I would have to revise my thoughts on the whole mailbox question.

At home I sat down to readdress the issue.

Dear Mrs. Barlow…

But no thoughts came. In fact, I wasn't feeling so well. My stomach was grumbling. I was hungry and suddenly impatient with the whole scenario—just who was this Mr. Hale? Wasn't I giving him too much credit? I sat, mulling it over. (*Hale*: free from infirmity, especially in an elderly person/to bring as by dragging; to haul a man to court.)

I pulled out my phone book. (Yes: I have a phone book; it was delivered to me by the Post Office, despite my lack of phone. One can count on their bureaucracy to keep them from noticing details, facts, even. Fact: Melanie Maddox does not buy into the Phone Company.)

There were lots of Hales (what did he do, sire 100 of them?), but not too many V.R.'s … I went down the list. The Mr., it turned out, lived on Creamery Hill. It took me almost an hour to remember where I'd put the map I'd gotten a few weeks ago—the pocket of my winter coat of course, next to the piece of bagel I hadn't finished, now ready for a museum collection—and an equally long while to find Creamery Hill. How many small roads there were: twisting and turning and intersecting into so many Y's and V's, like the varicose veins my mother had suffered from. At last I spotted it: Creamery Hill, and then my heart skipped a beat. Almost connecting with it, almost but not quite, since the road petered off before reaching anything, was a road I'd forgotten to remember: Idle Hour.

So Mr. Hale and Miss V. were in cahoots together. She really knew how to spoil everything. Just when I'd forgotten all about her.... I stared at the map longer, trying to make sense of it. There was Chestnut Hill, not too far from the Elementary School, and there was Mrs. Barlow's lonely road, Hooper Hill—on the other side of town as Creamery, yet her mailbox had suffered the same fate.... Interesting. I surveyed the map a good long while, trying to imprint the overall picture—its roads and hills—on my mind, though I had never been blessed with a photographic memory, not even for a second (of course I would have made it through college if I had—despite Miss V. and all of her machinations against me). Lacking a useful memory, I took a pen and made a mark wherever someone I knew lived. I went through the list, making neat little X's, until I came to Miss V.... I saw that I had no idea where she lived. Once I had, but now.... She'd exchanged that college town for this one—with no college in or near it—why? And just what were she and Mr. Hale busying themselves with? But then the inevitable came to me; I could no longer withstand it: V.R. Hale was no more a man than I was. V.R. Hale was Victoria Hale, plainly speaking: Miss V.

The pain in my stomach was suddenly stabbing me. I busied myself with a hot water bottle—an old rubber contraption I'd inherited from my Grandmother (the only thing she'd given me). I lay in bed with the hot water bottle lolling on top of my stomach. Miss V. was surely killing me. Who knew what hens she was hatching now? I tried hard to squelch all memories. The pain was shooting through me. I had never felt so tricked.

XI. Harris Tweed

Someone was following me.

It had happened before—in that other town when I used to go down and read the bus schedules and watch the passengers get on and off the buses—people going places: fat moms with their children, students with overloaded backpacks, scruffy old men. I'd noticed a man, completely unremarkable—grey-green suit, a thin little moustache—standing in the far corner when I sat down on one of those hard plastic little bus station seats and drank my coffee. He was still there when I started to chip off the styrofoam from my cup, making a neat little pile inside the cup, letting it swim in the shallow pool of cold coffee. At last I stood up. Sure enough he started to make his way toward me. I beat it out of there, lost him on a side street.

But he kept it up, for days and days and days, lurking somewhere in the shadows behind me as I walked.

He was Miss V.'s henchman. I didn't need a detective to tell me that. She'd hired him after accusing me of harassment: I was lurking about on her property, spying on her, phoning and then hanging up on her—she had all sorts of amusing and not-so amusing theories about me. I might have laughed (why would I want to hang around that swamp she lived next to? That spooky lake, her house that looked like an architectural nightmare?), but she went even further, far further than she should have. She'd been drinking too much coffee, hallucinating on swampy backwater, casting blame around to see wherever it would catch. She accused me of being solely responsible for the loss of her pet. The poor animal had disappeared, never to be seen again, and according to her, I knew just where.

The pet in question was a springer spaniel. She used to leave him tied up outside on her lawn when she went off to the classroom. She didn't seem to realize that springers need company and they especially like children. Miss V. had none. Obviously her dog had gone off in search of some. Company, that is. You can't leave an animal all day long by its lonesome while you go off drinking coffee, chatting in hallways, making accusations in the classroom, and then expect him to be there when you get back. Life just doesn't work that way. But of course Miss V. didn't see it like that. She was in no way responsible. Someone else was. And so she'd decided—quite randomly, it seemed to me—that this someone was me. Well, they say grief has to go somewhere, be transformed into something, in order for it to disappear. Blaming me was the shape her grief took. I didn't need any ten- or twelve-stepper to explain this to me. I knew all about it. But knowing this didn't make me forgive her. On the contrary. After all, she lay at the very root, the rotted-out root, of the ruin of my college career.

And now she was at it again. What did she think? I wanted her newest pet—a basset hound—Charlie, was it?

A ridiculous name for a ridiculous animal. But then she'd never been any good at naming. The last one had been Falco. Why subject a poor springer to that kind of nomenclature? If it's a falcon you want, then go ahead and get one. Falco indeed. Well, springers were bird dogs, she'd got that right at least. But her dog couldn't have caught a bird if he tried. And he never did. Try. He was a sorry animal starved for company, someone to stroke his back and scratch behind his ears. We were friends for a while. But dogs are boring finally. They can never give you the satisfaction a child can. A dog has a dog's life, after all, short and puny, and then you have that grief to contend with—something Miss V. was not at all up to. A child, on the other hand, almost always outlives you.

Sometimes the mind gets filled with calamities: He'd fallen out of bed and hit his head; someone smashed into him on the playground; a light bulb crashed and splintered and he needed 100 stitches on his forehead. My heart started to beat too quickly; I could feel the incredible yawning cavity of my life without Honda. Quickly I filled it back in again.

Let me describe him now, while he's sleeping. His eyelashes are beautiful: long, thin, dark, spider legs all in a row. He sleeps with his hands in soft fists, tucked under his chin, his knees brought up to his elbows. He looks extraordinarily peaceful. A child who isn't aware of his beauty. Which is as it should be. I myself was never beautiful as a child, less so as an adult, so it continually surprises me that my own child should be so extraordinary. On the other hand, why shouldn't I have something out of the ordinary to my name?

But now they were trying to take him—why else was a bronze Chevy cruising past my window? I watched him out the window. Her henchman. This one was not thin but fat, bulging, and balding. I was glad Honda was asleep—I didn't want him to have to see that. It was enough to give you nightmares, wide-awake ones.

Now he was parking, backing up his vehicle into a tight spot. He wasn't the smooth operator he pretended to be. His back wheel landed on the curb; he had to back down and try all over again. Now he was getting out, heading for the corner gas station/convenience shop. Minutes passed (what was he doing? Interrogating the attendant? Caught in a panic between caffeine and decaf?) before he exited at last, a cup of coffee in his gloved hand. Back in his vehicle, he sat sipping the coffee.

He reminded me of someone. His bulky size and nonchalant demeanor were reminiscent of a man I'd encountered some time ago…. And then there floated into view a dimly lit picture of a large individual who left his kid all alone while he ate his meals, ever so slowly, in various diners across the country. Just when was it decided that this same individual could block people's front view and engage in amateur sleuthing?

I caught sight of my own vehicle in the parking lot. The brakes were going. It was starting to be a dangerous undertaking. For instance, the little furry guy who suddenly makes a mad dash in front of your wheels—it was getting harder and harder to brake in time for him. The pedal now required a certain amount of pumping. You couldn't just press down on it, brimming over with confidence, like some people do.

I wondered where Pie Man had left his kid this time. I didn't see him in the back of the vehicle. The more I wondered about him—the kid—the more nervous I felt for him. My own predicament seemed minor in comparison. Who knew what this man was capable of? The gloves alone were cause for concern. Was he worried about fingerprints? The thing to do—I thought—was to somehow turn the tables on him. Follow after him.

That's when I remembered about the things I'd bought at Bargain Basement. I'd gotten a very nice man's suit, Harris Tweed I think it was, for just a couple of dollars. I didn't like going in there too often. The lady there always got that gleam—that helping-the-less-fortunate sense of satisfaction—when she sold me something. "Oh, that's a very good winter coat," she'd said, for instance, when I laid my new fur-lined corduroy jacket on the counter, "and at an excellent price. You can't beat that."

"Certainly not," I told her, "I'll probably make at least twice that much selling it at the college fair this weekend."

She looked at me with an "ouch, that hurts" look, which was easier to take than her earlier "aren't you lucky, haven't we helped you out" approach. On one occasion she even looked like she might cry. From disappointment. Thinking that you've helped someone and then finding out you have, but not at all in the way you anticipated—that hurts, I guess. But it was no concern of mine. There was no reason for her to draw premature conclusions. Assuming near-poverty on very little evidence. I didn't need her misguided judgment or so-called sympathy. It was worth very little, after all, dispensed so freely.

Occasionally I went so far as to buy some things for Honda: a button-down sweater with horses galloping across it, short checkered pants with suspenders.

"Oh, what darling clothes—aren't they sweet? Makes you want to buy them even when you don't have children...."

Just what was she trying to get at? That sort of commentary was even more outrageous. "These will look perfect on my son," I told her, then regretted it immediately. That helping-out-the-less-fortunate gleam was visiting her again.

"That's wonderful, just wonderful," she said. "I'm so happy for you."

When I laid the man's suit in Harris Tweed on the counter, her face lit up again. "And a very lucky gentleman it is who gets this suit ... why, it's hardly ever been worn, just feel this fabric.... Woven on the Harris Islands off of Scotland, I think it was ... see the label?" There was no need to get so worked up about it. "An excellent price too—what a good buy you've gotten yourself today." I waited for her to put it in a bag. The whole transaction was making me uneasy. Why bring Scotland into it? But then before I knew it, "Do you think the men in the Scotland Yard wear suits like these?" I was asking.

"What an extraordinary idea, well who knows? It just might be—it's something to think about, isn't it? Let's see, we had this old book on Scotland in the Book Bin, would you like to have a look?"

Before I could stop her, she'd gone over to the Book Bin and was rummaging through it.

"It's really not necessary," I told her.

But she didn't seem to hear me, kept right on digging and tossing as if I hadn't said a thing, "I know it's here, I saw it just the other day. Let's see ... ah, I believe this is the one we're looking for...." She held it up to the light as if it were an expensive bottle of wine of incomparable vintage, instead of a tattered blue book with a moldy stain on its cover.

"You must have this," she said. "You can learn all about Scotland...." She handed the book to me. *Modern Scotland* was the title. I opened it up. "Industrial Trouble," "Country Life," "Two Great Men," "The Local Authorities," were some of the chapter headings.

"Do take it," the lady was saying as she steered me by the elbow back to the counter. "Let me put it in with the rest of your purchase—a bonus," and then she winked, as if we were part of some great conspiracy.

"Well...," I said, "the truth is...," but I could see how pleased she was, how the transaction had not only made her feel useful, but had given her whole life deeper meaning, and I found myself mumbling "Thank you," and "Goodbye" and "Good Day," and all the rest of those standards one usually hears, though not from me.

Later I regretted that whole exchange, the way the lady had steered me around, pawned a completely useless book off on me (I'd looked up Scotland Yard in *Random*: the metropolitan police of London, England, it said, named after a street in London. Scotland itself, not to mention Modern Scotland, had nothing to do with it). I'd avoided the Bargain Basement ever since. Bargains indeed.

Now I tried to remember where I'd put the bag with that purchase. I didn't need the book—it was the suit I wanted.

XII. THE WORST OF WINTER

I tried it on. With the hem of the pants and the sleeves of the jacket rolled up, there was no denying that it was a perfect fit. I had a wool hat which I stuffed my hair into and pulled down over my ears. I thought I looked handsome. A British gentleman. Scottish, maybe.

Outside I walked at a normal pace, taking a moment to glance at the henchman nonchalantly. He was still sitting in his car, finishing off a cheese danish (now where had that come from?), licking flakes off his lips. I walked around his vehicle to my own in the parking lot behind him. It was a relief to get into my car, to sit behind the wheel, to absorb the air that had been trapped inside all day. I was in no hurry. I could wait as long as needed for him to make a move. Even longer.

Maybe he sensed he was being inspected; in any case he craned his neck around. I ducked down just in time. When I sat up, I noticed what a very good view I had of my apartment. I scrutinized the window, trying to see what I could of the dim interior. I suddenly remembered I'd left Honda asleep inside. What a terrible thing…. If only he'd wake up now, show his face at the window, I could motion for him to stay inside, to lock the doors, to lie on the floor and not to move. I watched the window nervously. If only…

I realized suddenly that Pie Man had pulled into traffic. How clever he was! To get me distracted, worried for Honda, then to pull out when I wouldn't see him…. Quickly I started up the engine. It took a few tries before the ignition caught and by the time I pulled onto the street, Pie Man was a number of cars ahead of me. Perhaps it was better this way. He wouldn't notice me on his tail. I felt good, I would have felt wonderful even, but for the nagging feeling I had about Honda. Leaving him alone like that. With small things to choke on, not knowing how to cook himself anything—what if he did turn on the stove? Would he remember to turn it off again? At that moment I thought I heard the faraway scream of a fire engine. At least Honda liked fire engines. He'd find it all very exciting. It was getting difficult to concentrate. I couldn't see the Chevy anywhere in front of me. Had he turned somewhere? It was hard to figure, because as far as I could recollect, we hadn't yet passed a turn off. I kept on driving. The cars ahead of me were ambling slowly. Somehow or other, he'd gotten away from me—how could that be? I waited until I reached someone's driveway, pulled in to back out again. I drove back the route I'd covered. Since when was he so good at disappearing? For a bulky guy he did seem to have a lot of leverage. I drove the other way out of town trying to spot him. I covered all the back roads on the look-out for him.

I must have driven for a long time, much longer than I'd planned to, without ever finding Pie Man or his boy, not even the slightest trace of them. Which was unsettling. But easily explained, it seemed to me, because when I got back to my apartment, there he stood at the door to my apartment with all of my belongings on the sidewalk—not so many, after all, it had been a furnished apartment.

Things didn't look very good—it's true—with all of my possessions in piles on the sidewalk—but I was worried for Honda. I decided to ignore Pie Man, sort of walk right past him.

"Miss, just where do you think you're going?"

I was surprised by this "Miss" business. Couldn't he recognize a gentleman when he saw one? Not being one himself, I guess he wasn't capable.

"Excuse me, sir," I said, going ahead with the gentlemanly approach to things, even in the face of disaster. (Isn't that what the British did? Scottish even?)

"You're not allowed inside," he said. "In case you haven't realized, lady, you're being evicted." He said that last word with a certain vicious emphasis: e-*vic*-ted, coming down hard on the second syllable. Later I looked it up: to expel a tenant by legal process. Well, there was nothing legal here.

I didn't care for his pronunciation. Still, I remained an unfazed gentleman. "Excuse me," I said again, "but I've forgotten something...." Had I really said that? Something instead of someone? How awful, inexcusable...

"You're not allowed in there. There's nothing up there anyway."

I tried to push my way past him. His bulk came in handy as he attempted to block me. "I have to get up there. You don't understand. I've left someone ... my son .... Let me up the stairs," I said the last with such command and insistence, that the bulky individual actually stood aside for me to pass him.

"There's no one up there. Go ahead—see for yourself," he called after me.

The room was bare except for lots of dust and the original furniture. Actually it didn't look so different from when my things were in it. "Honda!" I whispered, then louder, "Honda!" I could hear the steps of the hefty guy on the stairs, a certain thud, thud, thud, drawing nearer. I looked under the sofa, the bed, the only closet in the room. I checked the bathroom, the shower stall, the cabinets, even the space behind the toilet. It didn't matter where I looked; I found only clouds of dust, wads of paper and strands of hair. Where could he have gone with a man like that poking into everything?

"I can assure you, lady—there's no one in here."

"Yeah, thanks to you," I muttered. In my mind I was still searching—reviewing all possibilities: an air duct? The ceiling panels? Underneath some floorboards? "Honda," I whispered, then louder, even louder, I couldn't stop myself, "Honda! Honda!"

Pie Man stood in the doorway, arms folded over his hefty torso, listening. "It's not exactly my business, but if you really do have a son, you shouldn't have left him here all alone."

"You're one to talk, Mr...."

He pretended not to know what I was referring to, gave me a look of consternation mixed with confusion, a look he'd obviously practiced previously. He seemed to think the whole mix added up to the picture of innocence. Well, he didn't fool me. Not for a second. But why get started? Honda was never going to show himself with this henchman on the premises.

"I'm going to have to ask you to leave now..." was Pie Man's next contribution.

I didn't try to argue. It was all part of a larger plan, something Miss V. had hatched in her spare time, in her long summers off, now set into motion. And no amount of Positive Thinking or Argumentation was going to undo that. I'd learned that the last time.

I surveyed the apartment one last time, my eyes searching the corners, the cupboard shelves, anywhere I hadn't thought of. But of course, he was nowhere. Pie Man had seen to that.

Outside I felt strangely disoriented. I looked through the piles, taking only what was needed (not a whole lot, actually: my blankets and water bottle, *Random House*, my notebook, pens, a few clothes, things that'd been Honda's, and—for some reason—my bonus book from Bargain Basement).

"You're lucky the landlord waited until the worst of winter had passed. From what I'm told he could have evicted you a long time ago...."

Was that so? So now I was supposed to feel lucky, grateful even. And how did he know the worst had passed? Had he received word from above? "My dear human being, the Worst has now passed. Prepare yourself for a Change of Season...." Well, I knew better. Just when you think it's over: the skies spit enough snow to last five more seasons.

I put everything I wanted into the trunk of my car. Pie Man even offered to help me. Of course he was pleased at how quickly it was all moving along. Possibly he'd expected more resistance. Did he think I was going to fight over that crummy one-room apartment? As if I couldn't afford anything better.

"Help yourself," I said, indicating the rest of my belongings on the sidewalk, making an expansive gesture with my hand, my arm sweeping over the various objects I'd rejected—the chinaman selling balloons (I couldn't recall now where I'd found it), the pencils and pens I'd collected (nobody cares anymore when they lose them), the box of No. 9 spaghetti noodles, et cetera. "You're welcome to any of it," I called to him over my shoulder.

I noticed that various individuals had gathered to stare and ask questions. I turned the ignition over and over, my chances for a quick getaway diminishing with each try. I thought I could see Cindy Sorry and Miss A.—or was it V.?—among them. Pie Man was enjoying the attention. Never mind that he knew nothing at all of what he was talking about. Most likely this very instant he was expounding on the quality of life, the change of seasons, mothers who looked for their children under sofas. I could see his thick arms waving wildly, his mouth open and laughing, as he said whatever was needed to hold his small audience captive.

NOT a CHance

She was the kind of person who would find a small piece of glass in her sausage, take it out, and then keep on eating. Once we were having breakfast in a restaurant and her potatoes arrived with a fly on them. A dead one. She didn't think I saw it, I could tell. I pretended not to notice as she carefully flicked it to one side, then dropped it to the floor very quietly. I watched her eat her potatoes. I couldn't help thinking about it. I thought it disturbed her too, I saw her wince; she was having trouble finishing them. "Why don't you send them back? How can you go on eating them?"

"What?" she said. She really seemed at first not to know what I was referring to. "Oh well," she said. "It was just a fly. People are so squeamish." She smiled then.

It was her smile that did it, the way it seemed to come from some hidden reservoir, a light source almost—no,

I'm not explaining this well. It's that she wasn't beautiful; she was almost plain-looking, but when she smiled, it changed everything. It was a gift. She smiled and you felt warmed; you lost yourself a moment just looking at her. She caught you up in it and you suddenly wanted to be a part of her. It wasn't always like that. These were moments.

I see it now like that fly, or the speck of glass in her sausage. Anyone else would have stopped eating. Only she would go on to finish the sausage. There's something wrong about it. But she was like that. With him. Of course at first it wasn't noticeable. But eventually it was there: the fly, the speck of glass, the things about him that anyone else would have stopped at. He must have liked that about her: that she didn't stop, that she persisted. She loved him. At least she thought she did. But who am I to say she didn't? What is love after all, but an image we carry inside ourselves? She told me she loved him better than anyone else who'd ever lived. She thought they'd known each other in some other life; in fact, she was quite sure of it. But I'm jumping ahead.

She told me how they met. It was in Café Gaby's. She was writing when he came in. She worked as a translator and used to bring her work to the café. From the beginning she was very aware of him. He had a book, a thick book; he was reading from it and laughing. She wanted to ask him what it was. She couldn't see from where she was. But she couldn't make herself ask him. She was shy that way. And then since she wasn't going to talk to him, but could think of nothing else, she decided to leave. She hadn't seen him approaching. She thought he'd ask for matches. He asked for a piece of paper instead. She tore one from her notebook. It ripped and she had to start again. He stood looking at her. "Will you be here tomorrow so I can borrow more paper?" She laughed and said she would.

They met the next day. He told her he needed to learn Spanish; he still couldn't speak it very well. "What you need is a Mexican girlfriend," she said. "Let's see," she said, thinking of her own friends, "what kind of girls do you like?"

"Oh, someone like you," he said.

It made her laugh. I know she told him she was married. It didn't cost her anything to say she was. She still loved her husband, or thought she did. I saw that they were drifting apart even then, but I never thought they would leave each other. I thought they needed to take a vacation together, to sort of start all over. I think she thought so too; I know she used to, but when she met the American she gave up on everything. Not initially, but gradually, very gradually but definitively, until those of us who had known her found ourselves trying to avoid her.

But I've jumped ahead.

He left her—left Mexico, that is. They had a date in the café the day before he was leaving. She told me she got there late—maybe fifteen or twenty minutes—her boss had held her captive with a dictation. She arrived out of breath, running. She looked around for him but he wasn't there yet. She sat down and waited. The waiter arrived and handed her a folded piece of paper. It was a note from him. She told me what it said: "Remember what I said about keeping a distance with people I love"—something like that. I can't remember exactly. She told me she'd ripped it up into small pieces, dropped it in her coffee.

He didn't remember the note. That's what she told me. She thought it was funny: the words that had made her cry, that she'd turn over in her head, again and again…. He didn't remember writing them. "It sounds like something I'd have written…" was what he said. How could he not remember it? It made her laugh, though I can't see the humor in it. What he did remember was a letter she'd written him, a very short letter. She had an address for him, a post box somewhere in Arizona, and she'd written him a note, telling him about the weather and a weekend she'd gone on with her husband.

When he ran into her on the street again, almost a year since he'd seen her, maybe six or eight months since she'd sent the letter, the first thing he said was, "So you had a rainy summer?" She nodded. She couldn't believe she was seeing him again. But later he asked her: "Are you still married to a Mexican?"

She said that she was. "But not for long," she added. "I've decided to leave him…." She told me that it was a decision she'd made that very day, an hour or two before running into him.

It's not easy to get a divorce in Mexico. Her husband didn't want to give her one. He tried to understand what had happened but he really failed to. He used to ask me what it was, "Is it because he's American? But he's just a kid…." I think he thought she'd get over it and come back to him. That's what we all thought, actually. But even before their separation, before her husband knew anything, he met the kid. She had invited him over; she thought her husband could find a job for him.

She was very brazen about it. Of course her husband knew—just seeing how they looked at each other was enough to let him know they were itching to sleep together. But then because he was cautious, because he didn't want to accuse her unjustly, he waited until they left and watched them from the window. And he saw the way she kissed him. She did it fully on his lips; she didn't seem to realize or care that anyone in the world could see them.

He was furious. What did she take him for—*un pendejo*? Did she think him a complete fool? I saw that too: it was as if a part of her, the years they'd had together when she'd really loved him, were frozen up in her. It was that night that he raped her. Of course, he didn't use that expression—she did. He told me only that he'd forced her to have sex with him. He hadn't meant to. He wanted to make love to her and when she resisted, said she was sleepy, he got angry. "Why won't you have sex with your own husband? *¿Qué te pasa?*" he asked her.

"I just don't feel like it … I'm tired…."

"What makes you so tired? You've gotten enough already? Someone else has already laid it to you?"

He kept at her. She tried to struggle out from under him, but he thrust himself in and even though she cringed and cried out, it only made him try harder. With each thrust he drove her further away from him. He knew that; he knew then that he'd ruined any chance of getting her back again.

Later he apologized; he wanted a chance to start over. He asked for an explanation, "But why?" he asked her, "why him?" She couldn't explain it; maybe she didn't feel that she needed to. "We knew each other as children," she once said. "What? What are you talking about? You mean you knew each other before?" "Yes," she said, "but not literally…." He couldn't understand this. He asked me about it. I think he thought because I was part gringa (my mother was Canadian, my father Mexican) that I could explain it to him, but I couldn't explain it any better than she had. I think I even told him that she'd get over it.

She found a tiny square of an apartment in the city center. It didn't even have a phone. The few windows faced the courtyard where women did their laundry. It made me sad to see her there. But she liked it. All she cared about was that her husband give her the divorce papers. But he wouldn't do that for her. Not yet. He wasn't ready to.

It isn't easy to find an apartment as a woman alone in Mexico. They think they're renting to prostitutes. The sign had said: Apartment for rent. Married couples only. So she said she was married. And after all, she was. The lady didn't suspect anything. She rented her the room and only later met "the *señor.*" She must have known he wasn't really her husband—he'd be there for three days and then he'd disappear again. "My husband's a salesman, he does business in the States," she told the *portera*, which was a good explanation except the kid was clearly not a salesman. He was so obviously just that: a kid.

The first time they made love was when they decided they had met in another lifetime. I shouldn't say "decided," I should say "realized," since that was what she said. None of this part seems that important to me, but to her of course it was. She said he acted surprised that they were so passionate. I don't doubt that they were that: passionate in bed. And afterwards he said: "What did you say you were in your last life?"

"I didn't," she said.

"I thought you said you were a countess in France…."

"I did?"

"A countess, very beautiful. I think we knew each other then. But I wasn't noble; I was just a stable boy or something…."

Once decided on the story, they made love again.

She was like that, I guess, a romantic. She believed in things like coincidence. Birthdays, initials, numbers, and dates carried all sorts of meaning for her. And it was the same with him. She was forever telling me all the things they had in common, that their minds seemed to run parallel: how they'd meet somewhere in the city by accident, how they were always running into each other. She'd be walking and suddenly find him resting at the bus stop of a bus he wouldn't get on; sitting on a park bench talking to a shoeshine man. No, he didn't want his own shined. He liked the scuff marks. Yes, but once he'd let a cobbler fix his flapping shoe sole and he'd gotten a headache— those nails seemed to pound right into him as he walked…. This was what she told me: somehow her senses always led her to him. Not all of it was serendipitous; however, once she told me how he was always surprised to find her walking into the café just after he had (they never specified a time), when the truth was she'd sat in the library opposite, waiting and looking for him. So I'd have to say she engineered a lot of it.

There was one thing that was uncanny, however. And it says something about him, and why we tried to make her leave him. To begin with, he never had any money. She would lend him some, small installments, though she never outright supported him. They didn't want to do it that way. He had his own room somewhere and he'd find money where he could: an odd job, a relative in the States who sent him something; I really don't know what else he did.

It's hard to come by books in English and she had a lot of them. She had lent him some—maybe ten or twelve of her favorite ones. And that was that until one day she wandered into the British Bookstore. She was leafing through a book when she heard some commotion in the back. She saw a fellow in a rumpled overcoat through the open door, another overcoated man with him. She watched them. It was like watching a play; the man was acting. She realized he was selling used books, being dramatic about it, bargaining for better prices as he gesticulated wildly. His friend and the bookstore manager—his audience—were laughing. And suddenly she realized that this man, so frenzied and dramatic, was her lover. She stepped forward to greet him and then stopped. They were her books he was selling.

"You're selling my books!" she said, scooping them up off the table, not even glancing at the men. She picked out her favorites—maybe four or five of them—saying, "You can sell the rest of them. I'm keeping these ones," and clasped them to her, while the men (and even her lover seemed a stranger then) only stared at her. It was as if she'd just ruined a very good show. Even the store owner seemed to resent her.

She was upset when she told me. "But isn't it strange?" she kept saying. "I walked into the bookstore at the very moment when..."

I agreed that it was. "Maybe it's good that you caught him. If he'd sell your books, who knows how else he'd betray you?"

But she shook her head. "He couldn't have made much money ... I would have given him the money...." It seemed to hurt her more that he didn't just ask her for it.

"How can you trust him now?" I kept asking. "It scares me. He could do something to you..."

She smiled then, "Don't be silly. They're only books," and the way she said it reminded me of the fly I'd seen her flick aside in the restaurant.

It would have been one thing if he had loved her as she did him, but he didn't; he was forever evading her. I know that when she wasn't with him she was looking for him. In the end that's all she did: look for him. But she told me about one time—before the end—when they were together in the way that she wanted; she told me having that one time made everything else worth it.

They went to a town in Veracruz for the weekend. They took a bus there and stayed in an old hotel on a beach somewhere. She paid for everything. She came back looking very tan, burnt actually. She kept talking about the smell in Veracruz, the way plants smell: a fetid odor of green things rotting. She said she liked it. She said anywhere you went, any town or beach or patio or plaza, that smell was there. It was a good smell, dank and deep.

I thought she must be talking about sex. I didn't know what she was referring to. I figured the whole affair was going rotten—it was stinking—and she was in the putrid part of it.

But what does that mean really? I didn't want to imagine it. And isn't it true that when our friends need us most—when they're farthest gone—is when we pull back from them. If I had known—but she wasn't who I'd known before…. What was there to talk about with her after all? I didn't want to hear about the smell in Veracruz, about the kid selling her things or her litany of what made her love him. I started to avoid her. Which wasn't hard, of course, because our circles were not the same now. It was the same with her husband—once we occupied her world, but that world didn't exist anymore. It's only now that I can make an effort to imagine what it was like for her.

For instance, we know that the kid disappeared. It was shortly after their trip to Veracruz. Maybe that was his goodbye to her. Because he was always leaving her; his life consisted of deserting people before they deserted him. He didn't want to get hurt again. She explained this to me. It was because of his childhood, a very difficult one—complete with divorce and a mother who wanted to be rid of him. But who among us has not had a difficult childhood, tumultuous in its own way, but finally not so different from any other…. I thought she was making excuses for him.

So each time he left her in the morning while she still slept or kissed her on the lips outside the café or said goodbye to her in front of her apartment (no, tonight he couldn't come in … tomorrow maybe), he was practicing for the real one. She knew this and she lived in dread, never knowing if this goodbye, if this disappearance, was the last one.

I would think by the time he left she'd gotten whatever it was she'd wanted from him, that in some way she was satiated, even if it only meant knowing that he loved her—after all, he'd practiced leaving her for almost a year. I would think, in a way, it came as a relief: to have him finally gone after having been dragged through so many rehearsals.

But this is the part I find strange. After knowing this about him, knowing it well enough that she even told me: "He's going to leave me, I know he is, he's leaving soon…," and not only knowing it, but agreeing to it, agreeing to it as part of what it meant to be involved with him, after so much preparation; when the final departure came, she refused to accept it. She convinced herself he hadn't really left her.

I wouldn't have found this out, but her husband asked if I would tell her something. He wanted her to know that he'd get her the papers—he could see she wasn't coming back to him—and he couldn't get hold of her. He'd written her but she never answered. He thought it must be because she couldn't stand him; he asked me to speak for him. I said that I would. I felt guilty because I hadn't seen her; I'd barely spoken or even thought about her in two or three months—maybe longer.

I stopped by her apartment but no one answered. In the office where she did translations, they told me she hadn't been in for over a month; they assumed she'd found a different job … gotten sick or pregnant…. I went back to her apartment. I asked the *portera* about her; had she come and gone recently?

"No," she told me, "and she owes me rent … *de hecho*," she said, "is she really married? I have my doubts…. It was all right before, but now with the rent she owes …. *No queremos ser una casa de esas* … we can't have a house of disrepute here."

I paid through the month; I asked if she'd open the room. "It could possibly be arranged…." I gave her another bill and she told me to follow her.

I wasn't sure what I was looking for. The refrigerator was almost empty (but then, wasn't it always? She'd told me she stopped cooking when she left her husband) and there were tortillas and bread that'd gone moldy. Yet all her things seemed in place; I found her suitcase in the closet; it didn't look as though she'd packed up to go anywhere. A small sense of panic was growing inside me. I needed a clue, something to tell me where she'd gone, to reassure me she was still around….

"Is she coming back soon?" the *portera* was asking me.

I nodded, still gazing around the room. I glanced through the papers on her desk—letters and reports she'd translated—nothing that told me anything.

"Well, I hope so, I can't have an empty room…."

"What?" I said. I realized the *portera* was at my elbow. "Oh no," I said. "You can't rent the room. I know where she is. I'm bringing her back," as if I really did and would.

She nodded. I saw it was time for me to go. Whatever I'd come for, I hadn't found it.

I walked slowly from her apartment. The sky seemed to have whitened and the air felt dense to me, as if it were hiding something. I didn't even know where I was going; my feet seemed to be taking me somewhere on their own. And then I realized: of course, to Café Gaby's. It wasn't far from where she lived. She'd always spent so much time there….

It was dark and smoky inside the café; it always was, no matter what time of day. I took a seat near the window and ordered an espresso. It wasn't long before Gabriel approached me. "Your friend left this here—you know who I'm talking about, *la gringa*…. I was keeping it to give back to her, but I haven't seen her...." He handed me a tattered blue notebook I recognized as her own.

"When did you last see her?"

Gabriel shrugged. "I don't know ... maybe a month? Did she leave? I'm surprised she hasn't come back for this—I don't know, I can't read English, but I think it's her masterpiece," he winked at me. "You know, a great novel she was writing ... she was always writing in here.... You'll see that it gets to her?"

I nodded. I watched him walk away, then stop to greet someone else, another customer. My heart was beating as I held the notebook, as if in it I held the solution, as if a great mystery were going to be solved by it. I opened the tattered blue cover to look at the first page. I was quickly disappointed. It was filled with actuarial valuations and credit analyses, reports she had done for the company. What had I expected? Did I really believe she'd been doing any other kind of writing? Yet I felt cheated. I tried to see if she'd dated any of the reports, at least to know the last one she'd worked on. But none of them had dates; they were messy and filled with cross-outs; there didn't even seem to be a real order to them—in the middle of a letter of credit, she'd translated an insurance policy. There was even writing in the margins. How scrunched up and illegible her handwriting was! I read one, through the maze of cross-outs and lines that zigzagged through the margin. I thought it must be what I was looking for. I looked for others; there were four in all.

> *Last night he was wearing his shirt the color of ripe tomato and I saw his hands: long fingers, nicotine-stained, broken nails, and his laugh was like a waterfall, tumbling down over rocks, boulders. I tumbled with him into a still dark pool, found his mouth underwater.*

> *He showed me where he lives. It is dark like his mind, clothes are scattered like his thoughts, and the air smells of crusty socks, worn-out shoes. Here seasons*

are confused. We fall onto his bed and I feel his weight on top of me. His chin scrapes my cheek; my face burns under his.

The room seems to have lived through storms. Across the street the nightclub robs the dark with its bright lights and music, fluorescent green. Somewhere church bells chime the hour. I count eleven, twelve, thirteen—bury my face in his chest, my nose in his underarms. I taste onions: raw, bleeding. I trace the scars on his body—this one where he dove into a river and a tree trunk caught him. This one where he crashed his motorcycle. This one—when he was born.

Hollows of hunger. A place I hadn't known before. "These are places you must go," he tells me. It is dark and gnawing: a cave, hungry and black, to swallow us. Surely I will die here, or be left alone. He laughs. His laughter echoes in all of the rooms, takes me to a corner, a hard shell. I bump into walls, watch my body bruise. A pain: sharp through the roof of my mouth, through my abdomen, the sound teeth make when they grind ... but it's gone. The room, black but soft, envelops me: I am alone.

I felt like smoking, though I hadn't smoked in years. I asked the man at the next table for a cigarette; he lit it for me. It was a Delicado, which are not delicate at all, but what the hell; it tasted good. I inhaled deeply, watching the smoke blow out through my fingers. I went through the pages once more, very slowly and carefully. I was looking for other messages or signs, a drawing even, a single word. I'd read through the valuations and reports word for word, when I saw on the back inside cover some writing in pencil that had been smudged and smeared:

I can smell him: cigarettes and crusty socks, stained fingers and pale, pale skin, freckled and long fingers

and nails that haven't been cut, will be broken before
they are cut, a shirt that smells of sweat, days of sweat,
tangled hair, swamp hair underarms...

I ordered another espresso, sipping it as I reread. It reminded me of something.... What had she said? A smell of green things rotting.... What made her like it so? And what difference did it make, after all, that she'd liked the smell in Veracruz, that she liked the way the kid smelled.... It still meant nothing to me, gave me nothing more to go on than what I'd already found, yet I couldn't help feeling that there was something in it.

I used the phone across the street from the café to call her husband. "Did you ever go to Veracruz with your wife?"

"No...," he told me.

"Well, if she were to go by herself or with someone else, say, to a little beach town somewhere, where would she go—do you know?"

There was a long pause. "I remember something," he said. "She wanted me to go there with her.... I didn't want to—you know, being an American everything was new to her. But to me—Veracruz is ugly—they've got tar on the beaches from so many oil slicks there ... it's dirty, it's nothing like the Caribbean, or the Pacific...."

'You fool,' I wanted to say, 'why didn't you go with her?' Suddenly it all seemed his fault—if only he'd taken her, when she'd wanted him to.... "Where was it she wanted to go?"

"I can't remember—some little beach town..."

"I know that—but which one? Where?"

"All right, all right ... I'm thinking...."

I could hear him thinking. There was something slow about him, methodical. I'd never really seen him that way before, but I suddenly found him plodding, overly cautious....

"A little town below Tuxpan..."

"Below Tuxpan," I repeated. I was writing this down in her notebook.

"I can't recall the name—it had an old hotel there…"

"Yes," I interrupted, "that's the one—what's the name?"

"I don't know, I'm thinking. Look," he said. "You'll find it on a map, any decent map…. Why do you need to know?"

"She's gone," I told him. "She's disappeared."

There was silence on the other end of the line.

"So what does a town in Veracruz have to do with it?"

"I don't know, I'm not sure … I just feel it does, that's all."

Silence again. "Is she really gone?" he asked. "What do you mean, she disappeared? Didn't she just take a trip somewhere?"

"Yes," I said. "A trip somewhere. Leaving all of her things behind, not paying the rent in her apartment … saying goodbye to no one…."

"And you want to look in Veracruz?"

"Yes," I said, "I'm going there…."

I found myself on an ADO bus, watching the landscape through the window. I thought of her sitting as I was, eyes fixed on the window. Of course the kid was next to her, maybe leaning his weight against her shoulder. I wondered what the landscape said to her. The city with its endless suburbs had been left behind long ago; we were in the mountains now. Dry and dusty, they rose on one side of the road. The road snaked around the girth of them and every once in a while in the valley below, I'd see a group of scattered huts, and then a sign by the side of the road to announce the fact that they made up a town: San Juan, Naranjos, Chicontepec, or I'd see a sign and no houses at all, but a lonely dirt road forking off somewhere.

Then suddenly there were trees—whole forests of pine. A dense fog encircled us as we drove slowly through the pines. The air was crisp and cool. There was a slow and winding descent and when we finally emerged, it seemed to me (did she see it that way also?) it was like peeling off a husk to find the fruit within, moist and succulent, shining green—as if it'd been there all this time, whole and intact, waiting for you to lift it out and bite right into it. I opened the window as far as it would go and the air that came in was warm and balmy. I saw orange and lime groves, fields of stumpy trees with bright red berries—coffee plantations—and when the air grew denser and more humid, I watched the line of the sea grow near.

It wasn't hard to locate the hotel. It was old and rundown, but still had some of its former elegance; once it had been a resort hotel, and it wasn't hard to imagine women in white tennis outfits and men in shorts with tanned calves walking through the hallways. There was something antiquated about it, the feeling of a room in a museum which had been forgotten, an exhibit collecting dust and cobwebs, an exhibit of faded elegance—old wedding dresses, cognac glasses, and crystal chandeliers.

I studied the contents of a glass case in the hotel lobby: a stuffed armadillo, a set of shark's teeth, and a marlin; a bottle of vanilla and a package of vanilla-leaf cigarettes— "products of the region," according to a hand-lettered sign. I rang the bell on the desk and a young girl came out of a room behind me, ducked under the desk and brought out an enormous guest book which she spread before me. "Sign here," she said.

I turned back the pages of the book—when had she come? June? July? No, no—the end of May. There it was: her name and address, the room number.

"Can I have room 109?" I asked.

She looked at me, eyes narrowed, "You're lucky there's any room at all. We were full last night." She turned to reach for the key and I saw that nearly all the keys were there, hanging from numbered hooks.

The room was clean, with a neatly made bed, a view of the ocean through the bougainvillea outside the window. I stretched out on the bed and closed my eyes. I could hear the ocean, the waves crashing in rhythmic succession against the shore. They lulled me; I felt suddenly peaceful, almost as if I were lying on the sand and the waves were inches away from me.

I woke up to a vision of them (or was I asleep, dreaming?): he was making love to her. Sunburnt and naked, their bodies fit together like a strange sea animal—a crab with its shell removed—thrashing on the bed, breathing hard. I felt that it was hurting her, chafing her where their reddened skin rubbed, almost burned, but they kept on. I thought I heard her asking him to—to keep on, to thrust harder, deeper; I thought she was asking him to obliterate her.

I went into the bathroom and splashed cold water on my face. I let the water run for a long time as I tried to rub the image out from behind my eyes.

I had a photo of her with me—one of those photo machine strips we'd taken together some time ago—she was looking straight at the camera, a warmth around the eyes. I took it with me as I made the rounds the next morning: the beach, the small town and its plaza, the shops along the outskirts. "Have you seen this person?" I asked the women who ran the restaurants, the girl at the souvenir stand, the man who raked the beaches clean. But no one remembered her. Only a boy who found me first on the beach and then at the souvenir shop, who wanted to sell his services as a guide to some nearby pyramids (*¿Quiere ver las ruinas? Yo la llevo...*), said that he'd seen her. *"Le veía con un güero,"* a light-skinned guy, *"muy enamorados,"* and he mimicked kissing and hugging for me to illustrate his words.

"When?"

"Oh, two, three weeks ago...."

It couldn't have been them—unless he was confused about the time? But how could I count what a ten-year-old who wanted my money said as truthful? "What were they doing? Where did you see them?"

He shrugged. "On the beach, they were always on the beach, always together, *eran novios, pues. No querían ir conmigo."* They didn't want his services.

Later, sitting on a bench in the plaza, I thought I could smell what she had: the smell of dark wet earth, of green things rotting. It wasn't a bad smell.... For a while I sat drinking in that smell, fingering her notebook. It was worn and thin, not the thickness of the 100 *hojas papel bond* she'd bought. I tried to imagine what was written on the pages she'd torn out, pages of writing which had nothing at all to do with her job. If only I had them...

There was nothing to do but to read through it again. I knew that I'd already read every line, but it was all I had of her. There was still the chance I'd see something. And at last I did find something—a very small something. It was scrawled in pencil, very lightly, or so I thought initially, until I realized it was only the impression of a pen pressed down hard on a page now gone. The handwriting was different from hers, more spindly, and at the same time, squatter: *Not a Chance, not a chance, forgotten romance...*

They were his words, words he'd told himself over and over: he wasn't going to fall in love with her, wasn't going to let himself. No matter how much he felt the force of her love, an undertow pulling at him.... And she knew he was battling against it, trying hard not to succumb, standing still in the ocean, resisting the wave's pull.

I was picturing them, imagining their end with eyes half-closed, when a voice interrupted. "Pssst. *Güerita."* It was the boy Manuel. He was out of breath from running, his eyes full of excitement, *"Oiga...Me equivoqué...Sí, los llevé a las ruinas....* It was a rainy day, they couldn't stay on the beach, they went with me instead, we took three buses to get there. I'll show you. If you want, we can go there."

What was the point? If he had taken them, why hadn't he remembered them before? Wasn't it just a tale to get me to employ him? I made him describe her again, and the kid too; the details he gave (her yellow bathing suit,

the kid's red-brown hair) felt accurate—or maybe that was
how all tourists looked and dressed in this beach town.

"All right, you'll show me then."

Manuel grinned.

The bus was small and crowded, the road dusty and
full of holes. I tried to imagine them on the bus with him;
it had been rainy, he said, not the afternoon sun that we
had. Every so often Manuel would make a comment,
"She's your sister or friend? *Era muy bonita...*"

The last bus let us off at the foot of a dirt road which
took us to the ruins. I realized that in different circumstances I'd be hearing Manuel tell about the history of the
area, the Totonaca Indians, the design and structure of the
pyramids. Now he was reconstructing the story of my
friend. Was it memory or imagination he was drawing
from?

"Since it was cold that day, and they weren't dressed
warmly enough, she was always holding onto him, to get
warm, I think...," he watched me for my reaction. "They
bought me *tamarindo* candy from the vendors," he ges-
tured to the girls carrying baskets of *tamarindo* and plan-
tain chips in plastic bags. (I took that as a sign I should
buy him some, and paid a young girl who'd been following us.) *"Eran bastante generosos, quiero decir, ella era.* It was
she who paid for everything...." I nodded; it sounded just
like her.

Though the site was small and little-known, the ruins
were impressive, unlike any I'd visited. Neither Aztec nor
Mayan, they were built like crumbling wedding cakes,
each tier a layer of *nichos,* small windows. The largest pyramid numbered 364 *nichos,* Manuel told me (having slipped
into his repertoire), which with two more now gone from
the top, corresponded to the days of the year. We saw the
ball court, the *gran plaza,* but what intrigued me most was
the way the jungle encroached on the buildings; not long
ago it had covered them all and still there were mounds in
the distance, clumpy hills, pyramids the jungle refused to
yield.

"Follow me," my guide said, "I want to show you something." We climbed to the top of the farthest pyramid, from where to one side we had a view of steep hills and to the other, the horizon seemed to meet the ocean. "It was up here that I saw him push her, you know, pretending to push her off. He was joking, but she didn't like it. And then, when we walked back she wouldn't talk to him."

"Is that true?"

"*Claro.* Of course it is. *No voy a inventarlo,*" he said, sounding much too old and serious for a ten-year-old. "He tried to take her arm but she refused it. But later on the bus, on the way home, she sat on his lap, you know because there weren't enough seats. I stood of course. *La verdad, señorita,* is that I didn't trust him."

"Why?" I asked. We had descended the pyramid and were making our way down the dirt road we'd walked in on.

"*Le voy a decir una cosa,*" my guide said, watching me as he spoke. "*Se podía ver que él no era para ella,* she wasn't meant for him. *Ella era mucho mas fina, y él* ... he didn't know how to treat her. He shouldn't have let her pay for things, I would never let *mi novia* do that, of course I let you buy me things, but that's different, because I'm working for you, and anyway, you have lots of money," he smiled at me, "but with her ... he didn't act like a real man."

"Yes, but American men are like that—women pay, men pay—it doesn't mean anything."

"I've seen lots of Americans. *Ellos son mis clientes pues,* they're my customers. He was different. I could see something bad was going to happen to her because of him."

"But what are you talking about?"

He shrugged. We were waiting for the bus now, the first of our caravan-like trek of three buses back.

"You can't just say something like that and drop it."

He seemed to study me. "What can I say? But if your friend has disappeared, *la selva lo rodea todo,* there's jungle on all sides.... No one would know where to find her.... Or who would be responsible."

I stared at him. "You're being ridiculous," I told him. He shrugged, seemed to almost grin. Our bus had arrived and we boarded. We found seats (not like her, when she'd sat on his lap) though not together. I was tired after the sun, the travelling and exploring, and despite the noise, diesel fumes and constant bumping, I slid into sleep. On our second bus Manuel told me he wouldn't be taking the last one. He didn't live in the beach town but in Poza Rica, the oil-town that lay inland. He would get off there. "*Señorita*, I've told you all I know and observed. I hope it's been of help to you.... And I wish you luck finding your friend," he added, then lowered his eyes, as if—it seemed to me—he knew it to be impossible now. I paid him, adding a generous tip.

I had another bus ride, more comfortable but much longer, to face the next day. I tried not to think about it. There was the problem of what the boy had said. If there was anything at all in what he'd told me, I should be going to the police, asking questions.... But hadn't I already made a fool of myself, believing the smallest things he'd said? After all, I'd seen her in the city after her trip to Veracruz; it wasn't as if she'd never returned.... "*La selva lo rodea todo*, there's jungle on all sides. No one would know where to find her." I closed my eyes, shook my head. I'd been paying him to give me stories.

I ate in the hotel restaurant despite the higher prices and less authentic cuisine, showered, and went to bed. I don't remember having dreamed anything.

I spoke with her *portera*, no, *la güera* had not returned to her apartment. ("I've been watching, *he sido muy vigilante*," she told me, and I knew to believe her.) I made my way to Café Gaby's, sat again in the dimly lit room. I watched the other customers, half-expecting a ghostly face to appear, peering in at the window. I still had her notebook and every so often I lifted the cover to stare at its scrawled pages, as if its contents weren't already etched into me, actuarial notations and all. In a few moments I would use the phone across the street to call her husband, confess how fruitless the trip had been. I sipped my café espresso, lit a Delicado (I'd gone back to smoking them).

Whatever thread I'd been following was worn thin now. I'd let myself get off track, following scents and listening to stories. At the same time, I'd felt closer to her in Veracruz—I'd felt her presence in the hotel room, on the beach and in the plaza. I knew that their weekend together in Veracruz—the ocean, the sun, their fevered love-making—had been their last one. Hadn't she told me he wouldn't spend the night with her on their return, choosing his own room on the other side of the *centro* instead? In the morning she went to find him. The *portera* insisted he was gone, but she thought she saw him standing behind the curtained windows of his apartment. He was avoiding her. Hours later she would try again. And again. And then the blue curtains disappeared—the ones she'd given him to drape his windows with—white lace in their place. But no one would tell her where he'd gone, what had happened to him.

The talk of the other customers buzzed around me, occasional laughter and some spirited shouting. The old man selling lottery tickets made his way between chairs, stopping to rest at each table. "*La suerte, la suerte,* try your luck," he said. I bought two tickets, "*Gracias, güerita,*" he said.

"*¿Te acuerdas de la otra güerita?*" I heard a voice somewhere behind me—low, hushed, "Remember the other light-skinned girl who used to come here? *Pobrecita.* I saw her the other day over by Plaza Neza, so skinny, skinny and white as paste … her clothes like rags and her eyes … just empty pools—they didn't seem capable of recognizing me, or anyone…. I tried to give her something, but she wouldn't take it from me—*¿Tu crees?* Can you believe it?"

My skin prickled and I suddenly started coughing, a cough that wracked me. I wiped my eyes and turned to ask the two women, "Was it her? Are you sure? Where is she?" But no one sat at the table behind me.

Somehow, so quickly, they'd made their way out of the café. I gathered my things, left some pesos on the table.

I walked quickly, my heart like a small fish, jerking and leaping inside me. It was a long way to Plaza Neza—would she be there as they'd said? I searched the faces of people who jostled past me, but they gave away nothing. I scanned each street I came to, the side streets and alleys, the intersections I had to stand at to wait for traffic to pass. I took in whole streets at a time, as if in one glance I could canvass every single face to find the one I wanted. Avenida Juarez. Bucareli. General Prim. Faces swirled past me. I walked faster.

On certain days she must have caught a glimpse of him—how else could she go on believing? She must have thought she'd seen him—his uncombed hair, the tail of his red shirt flapping after him—only to rush after this image and find that her mind had played tricks on her again. Streets she'd once walked with him, streets where she'd often found him, seemed to be holding back from her now, as if they knew something but would never reveal it. Balderas. Ayuntamiento. Cinco de Mayo. La Calle Uruguay. The city seemed an endless labyrinth, an impossible maze of streets. There must be someone to ask: Isn't this the way to Plaza Neza? For a second it seemed there was no one. On the opposite side of the street was a bakery; I made my way over.

When the car brushed my thigh, its driver screaming, What the hell do you think you're doing, don't you have eyes? What are they for then?, it took me some moments to realize she might have been hit, might have been hurt. I knew that as she walked she told herself she didn't care; didn't care at all what happened to her. She walked with no thought to where she was going; she walked because it seemed the only thing she knew how to do; she walked and walked as if her feet slapping the cracked uneven pavement were her only answer.

But her leg pained her. Was it broken or only bruised? What did it matter, except that walking had become too painful. And walking had been her refuge. She rested on the sloping steps of a stone building, leaned against the wood door and closed her eyes. The sound of traffic, of so many feet and voices scurried past her, like mice tracing escape routes. She felt herself sinking deeper into darkness.

It was still dark when she woke. She was cold, but not enough to numb the throbbing in her leg. She saw that she was lying in the corner of a large and empty room. A shawl had been wrapped around her; a *bolillo,* a bread roll, set beside her. Her cheek touched the cold of the stone floor; she wrapped herself tighter. A bird flapped its wings and resettled itself in the darkness. From the vaulted ceiling she thought she could hear his laughter.

Dead End

Dear Jacobo:

In your very private space a man is spying on you, watching you get up, make your Turkish coffee, sit down to drink it as you read the paper. He sees you at night as you check your machine and call into the one in the office, "just to make sure no one's threatening suicide." (I'm not surprised Bonita tried after all, with you how could anyone ever achieve a feeling of safety?) He sees you as you flip on the TV, as you watch the videos you selected from the back, the small red room; he watches you masturbate to *Jacuzzi Suzy*—no, it doesn't fill him with any sense of participatory pleasure; he is not a voyeur, he's nothing but a hitman setting his sights. When will he strike? I've left that up to him, he's a professional, I'm sure he'll do it when and how it's meant to be done. "I'm bringing out your aggression," you used to tell me, so all of this must be making you very happy. Don't think that didn't cross my mind. I thought: why give him the satisfaction of knowing he's been successful? But other instincts took over, maybe an ounce, just a quarter of a gram of feeling, though it's true, any number of memories could eliminate even this small bit of empathy for you— any number of memories can make me want to pull the trigger myself, but then—and how can I explain this to you?—some feeling of human decency takes over, and it seems much better to have hired someone else. And I do want to warn you—let me remind you again—there's a gun pointed straight at your head, and a man behind it, aware of the slightest move you make. Don't try to outguess him or track me down, either way you'll come to a dead end…. And I do mean the pun I just made without even trying, yes, other people besides yourself are capable of cleverness. But no one more than the man I've hired.

Allow me the pleasure of dropping one hint: I think he intends to get you while you're sleeping. He confessed this to me when we made arrangements in a seedy downtown diner and it was the one time a thin crevice of doubt opened up inside me, seeing the glint in his brown eyes, together with the crispness of his white collar, grey suit jacket; there was something cruelly mathematical about him, but then I reminded myself that was why I hired him, why he came recommended and the tiny crevice healed nicely (don't even ask how I found him, don't waste your ninety dollars per fifty minutes—your $1.80 per minute time). He'd been staring into his watery black coffee when he looked up and told me: It's the look of blood on a pillow, the sweet smell of sleep still lingering. I guess you could say it's my trademark. To be shot through while dreaming....

I'm not afraid to admit that once your sleeping face looked beautiful to me, the morning after our first night together—when I woke and saw through your window the green of clinging ivy, heard the chirp of birds (how unexpectedly quiet and peaceful, I remember thinking), felt a gentle happiness spreading through me, moving slowly but thickly like an overturned jar of honey, until all my senses were coated and I wanted to kiss you awake, but held back— scenes from the night before still flashing. We hadn't made love yet, you told me you weren't feeling desirous of me but sleepy (you were angry again that I wasn't talking: You're so interesting over the phone, you have so much to say, and in person you're so quiet, pretty boring— why is that?), but I had the image of your penis pointing toward me, bumping against me at various times during the night while you slept unaware of its aroused state, a weathervane of your desire, I thought. I hadn't slept soundly, had woken often and stared at your closed eyes, heard your soft breathing and felt the wonder of lying naked next to a man I knew only slightly, in a studio apartment in Manhattan in a bed not too far from the kitchen table. The strangeness and familiarity of the room: VCR, books, sofa, bed, photos I wanted to examine and scraps of paper with writing I wanted to read. We wrote each other letters in the morning after making love (an act that was over almost as soon as it started, but it was, after all, our first time I told myself then—ha) and I was surprised at the frankness with which we wrote, but even then your letter was suspect. Certainly it was written by you, but was it really meant for *me*? Couldn't it have been anyone, anyone you'd just spent the night with? Don't you remember that time I visited you in your office (and this was weeks later), and the janitor stopped in and you wanted to impress me—you were friends with people even of his low stature—and him—here was your leading lady, wasn't she attractive?—but when you went to introduce us, you'd forgotten my name. How could you forget my name? Was I no one to you, or any one at all—? Or do you just forget things ... well, now you have a chance, a once in a lifetime chance, to forget everything: it can all go out through the hole in your head. Memories and pain too—think of all the pain you'll be able to rid yourself of, all that pain you screamed at me about; I could never really understand how it was for you.

Out the hole: men hanging, necks in a noose, all in a row

Out the hole: your house with the beautiful garden—burned, gutted out

Out the hole: the boy who always beat you up after school

Your father who never took you to the zoo, never paid attention to you

Your mother spooning you food, not letting you feed yourself, until you were ten years old

Your old girlfriend in Philadelphia who broke it off with you

...

I realize this isn't even a fraction of the list, the real list that I can never know, being younger,

American, not Jewish, but most of all, not *you*. But put this way, it seems I'm doing you a great favor, one you'd thank me for if you knew how to find me ... but you won't. I've moved and have an unlisted phone number. I don't even live in New Jersey anymore. Am I in your beloved Manhattan? Not saying. You won't find me. I go to none of the restaurants we went to together, not that one in midtown where you suddenly showered parmesan cheese on my head (why, I can't remember, but of course not before you'd chanted, "You understand *nothing!*"). I never go to that park we used to sit in, where even the trees shuddered at your screaming, while the rocks identified with me. Or the beach we'd go to in the middle of a weekday—I never go on a Tuesday or Wednesday—and I don't walk all the way to the end where gays hang out like we used to. I go with a man who never complains about the quality of my conversation, who doesn't ask to be masturbated while others pretend not to be watching, who never caresses my nipples for hours then suddenly stops, without making love to me, leaving me hungering. You won't run into me. I avoid the street where your office is—once I walked the forty blocks from 14th Street just because I wanted to, I was happy to walk all those streets to reach you—now I make sure I have no reason to go near. I am not who I was with you, I do not get screamed at in public or private places and there are always things to talk about and lots of sex that is satisfying and long-lasting....

But I've gotten off track. The thing you must remember is: across from the place where you live looking straight into the window above your bed is a man with an Armalite 180 aimed straight for your head. He's watching you now as you read this, as your eyes look to the window and down at the page again, he sees you as you slouch back into your plush grey sofa, letter falling to the cushion beside you. He feels the give in the trigger, he lets the pad of his finger rest there before he pulls—but no, he'll wait, wait til you're undressed and lying in bed, when your eyelids droop and the tension has gone from your forehead, your cheeks relaxed, your breathing steady; you look just like a newborn when you're sleeping.

Nicaraguan Birds

We met her in Mexico City. My husband didn't like her. He said that her energy tired him and it's true; one felt tired just watching her, but she required listening as well. She'd quote Marx, Hegel, Freud, Erikson, Perls, but her hero was Gramsci. She'd made a pilgrimage to the island of Sardinia, where he was born, and she couldn't even count the times she'd read his book, *Prison Letters*; "Can you imagine the founder of the Italian Communist party sitting in prison for eleven years?" The blue of her eyes seemed to deepen when she spoke of him and her hands, which were constantly shaping words—summoning them like birds fluttering around or above her, or thudding onto the table before her—seemed to tense as well. She fidgeted with her rings; there were three. She took them off, one by one, fit them on different fingers, all on one finger, into a triangle on the table. Her hair was long and blonde in a time when women wore theirs short and somewhat styled. And she dressed in Mexican peasant dresses, unaware they were no longer in fashion. But then she'd been in Latin America an awfully long time, and what did she care what wealthy people wore? Her life work was for the oppressed and poverty-stricken. She'd been all over Central and South America, and in the poorest barrios. She'd seen houses made out of sheets of milk carton, junkyards for neighborhoods, families of ten, twelve, thirteen living in one room. But things were going to change. Sometimes she couldn't sleep, thinking of all the work that had to be done—organizing, rebuilding, forming cooperatives; it had to be started now. She was ready; what was she waiting for?

My husband, with little patience for her brand of politics, stopped listening to her. At first he had listened in order to argue. But she would pounce on his one or two lines—he was still working up to a rebuttal—and out would come another torrent of words. It was impossible to argue with her. She lost you in her logic. And she spoke with a tremendous speed, even in a language that wasn't her own. Perhaps she was afraid we'd never stay to hear it all if she spoke at a normal pace. Or perhaps it was only urgency that propelled her hands and words.

I was helping her correct an article in English—her theory on the role of the individual in social change—for a symposium. The first draft was lost in Colombia when her bag was stolen, the second in the mail between England and Germany. She had reconstructed it from memory. The paper was very long and scribbled across the backs of old letters and Xeroxes.

My husband didn't see why I continued to work for her. He himself was a translator for a large publishing house in Mexico. His Spanish was flawless. My own Spanish was good, but never quite as good as his. He sometimes gave me things to work on—letters and articles, writing that didn't have to do with the creative side of novels; he said I needed first of all to fine-tune my Spanish. Every so often I did freelance work for a small company: insurance and banking, all very technical—something my husband looked down on. "Why waste your talent on an actuarial valuation or a financial statement? Why not wait until at least a good television script comes along?" He urged me to stop working for Karla—I wasn't getting paid; her prose ("if you can call it that") was tedious.

I thought I would give notice the next time she called, but instead I accepted "just a few more pages." I corrected the grammar, her syntax, her choice of words, so that all her sentences ran smoothly together like thoughts when we are half-sleeping. But I didn't understand the paper. The language was obtuse; it seemed to walk under, over and around, but never into her ideas. Every few paragraphs there was a quote from Hegel, Gramsci, or Freud.

Each time we met she offered me small gifts, always wrapped in paper napkins. First it was a handful of cookies and a tablespoon of coffee. Then there were small twigs and berries in a pottery jar. And then two straw birds made by children in Matagalpa, Nicaragua. Frayed at the edges and a little dusty, they looked as though they'd been hanging on her own apartment wall. I imagined her digging through her few possessions, trying to find something suitable to offer me. Soon her poor apartment would be bare; she'd have no more earrings, plants, decorations to give me. I tried to refuse the gifts, but this offended her deeply; they were humble, small details only, but didn't I like them? I had to show her where I'd hung the birds; I wore the earrings whenever she came by.

When I gave her the pages I'd revised, she seemed overjoyed. She hugged me and kissed me on the cheek. She was tall and smelled of perfume. Perfume wasn't something I associated with revolutionaries, but perhaps it was her European background. The house smelled like perfume long after she'd gone: a little too sweet, a little too strong.

She'd been coming and going for two weeks before my husband asked me: "Is that some new perfume you're wearing?" He'd kissed me too, having just got home.

"Oh no," I told him, "That's Karla's. She wears so much you know."

"You mean you're still working with Karla?" He had an even-tone way of speaking which sometimes masked what he was feeling. I told him just until we finished the article, not much longer. "I didn't know exploitation appealed to you." He was trying out sarcasm. It didn't suit him.

Perhaps Karla knew he didn't like her. The first time she came to work with me, she looked around the apartment timidly. "You're alone?" When I told her I was, she looked relieved—no, almost pleased. We drank coffee before starting the work together. If I offered her food—some cookies, a sandwich, a piece of toast even—she refused. But coffee she drank lots of.

She thought I was extremely intelligent. My choice of words delighted her; the way I understood what she was trying to express, and so quickly! She said these things at least once during a session of working together, as if she'd forgotten she'd told me before. I denied her praise emphatically; English was my language, rearranging the words she'd labored over came easily to me. Yet I looked forward to hearing her praise. It was another one of her gifts, like the straw birds and owl earrings (because I was wise, she said). I waited to see what she would bring me each time.

"Where did these come from?" My husband had an amazing capacity not to see something new I'd bought or was wearing—a pair of shoes, a dress even—until at least a week had gone by. Then quite suddenly he saw it for the first time. So it was with the birds.

"Oh … some Nicaraguan children made them. Aren't they pretty?"

"Hmmm," he said. He was lifting up the lid from a pot on the stove, wanting to see what I'd made for dinner.

The birds were not very pretty really. Or only in a primitive way. They were made of lacquered burlap and straw. It looked as if the children had one pattern to follow—the two were exactly the same, as much as handmade crafts can be. They gave me a depressing feeling—muddy brown like their color, not how I imagined Nicaraguan birds at all. But I knew Karla treasured them, and I appreciated her sacrifice in giving them to me. No, it was more than that. I felt she was trying to reach me with them, in a way perhaps no one else had. As if she knew something about me that I myself was still learning.

We were nearing the end of the article. It seemed to me that it was much too long, even for a symposium, but I shoved the thought from my mind. My task was to revise it, not rewrite it. Still I felt sad that it was all coming to an end—what we'd worked so hard on—and I spent long hours on the last ten pages. I wanted the conclusion to be particularly strong. I told myself it was only because I wasn't a Marxist psychologist that it made little sense to me, except grammatically. There seemed to be too many threads of thought, all tangled together in one stringy knot, and at the same time, it seemed to be the same two or three ideas repeated endlessly. The diagram she'd made to clarify the main points only increased my confusion, with its arrows and lines crisscrossing the page. I devoted all my time to those pages. But there was a deadline. When Karla called, I reluctantly pronounced it finished.

She seemed a mixture of happy and sad. Soon she'd be off to Nicaragua. She had an envelope with her; she pressed it into my hand. "I'm going to call you tomorrow." She kissed me on the cheek and was gone.

The money slipped out as soon as I opened the card. It was a thousand peso note, equivalent to five dollars, but that cheapens it greatly. Thinking in pesos, it came to a lot more. But I was thinking neither in terms of pesos nor dollars, but in Karla's terms, and for her it was a great deal of money.

I read the card. She thanked me for all my help; it was invaluable to her. She said she'd come to cherish me and wanted me to join her in Nicaragua. She said I would be of great help there, and especially to her, who needed someone whose steady intelligence could balance her fits and starts of nervous energy.

What I read both surprised and pleased me. I thought about her offer for a very long time. I tried to be rational and intelligent, qualities she admired me for. But part of me just wanted to go there with her and not think it over at all. That part of me made the decision.

I took out a suitcase from the hall closet, the smallest I could find, and started packing. What sort of clothes does one wear in Nicaragua? Light, yet strong and practical. A pair of sandals and walking shoes. My blue dress, green sweater, black slacks, and favorite t-shirts. I felt weightless suddenly: no furniture, no dishes, no rugs or carpets, though these were things I'd spent a good deal of time searching and bargaining for in open-air markets. I'd always been told how good my eye was, how my skill at bartering was something to be proud of. How odd that none of that mattered to me now. I wanted only the necessities: toothbrush, a few clothes, some books—two or three choice ones. I began to look through my collection. A novel by Márquez I hadn't yet read, one by Cela.... And what about my dictionaries—those thick books which had helped us so often. (Karla had only a pocket one someone had lent her.) I decided against them: much too heavy and cumbersome. Anyway my husband could send them later, if we needed them.

My husband. I'd been trying not to think of him. What would he say? (What would I?)

I let him open the door and kiss me before I told him. I hadn't forgotten to make dinner. He was looking into the soup pot. "Oh?" he said. I could see he wasn't listening.

"I'm going with Karla to Nicaragua," I repeated, more slowly and forcefully the second time. I waited for the meaning of my words to sink in. These were not just words; this wasn't a case of dreaming out loud.

"What?" he said. And then with his peculiar sense of timing, "Now wait a minute, since when have *you* cared about revolution? Or what is it you're interested in—? Not Karla—?"

I ignored his questions. I didn't want to get sidetracked. "I've packed a small suitcase," I told him. "But I won't be taking my dictionaries. Maybe you could send them later on…?"

This is when the phone rang. It was Karla. She wanted to know what I'd decided. I watched my husband as I spoke. "I'm going with you."

"Oh! That's wonderful! I'm so happy, I was hoping…"

My husband was glaring at me. Then he softened and laughed. "This is very amusing, you're doing so well. When do I get to clap?"

"It must have been difficult to make the decision, yes? I really didn't expect … I mean in your case, for me it's the only thing to do, but I mean, well, let's say you're more tied to the material … and your husband, well that makes it difficult too…."

"Does this mean you don't want me to?" I was getting confused.

"No, no, not at all, it's just that…"

I couldn't catch what she'd said; she was talking extra fast again. My husband seemed to be practicing x-ray hearing, which was disconcerting. "There are some things to consider," I heard her telling me. "You need to be prepared. You must start attending the meetings with Rafael, Luis, and Estela … I told you about them…. You also need to do some reading…"

"Yes, I know, I've packed some books…."

"Yes, very good, Luis will give you a reading list. No, better you get the books from him. He can drop them by your house. Also, there's a course I think you should attend. Not at the University—it's taught by El Habanero. In his apartment: Tamaulipas 224—are you writing this down? In the Colonia Condesa—you see, not so far from where you live. It will be very good for you. Excellent, really. He will absolutely change your thinking. I'm going to go on ahead and then you'll meet up with me, we can say in two, three months? Or do you think you need five months to prepare yourself?"

"I really don't know … I'm getting confused…"

"Of course you are," she told me, "but only right now. With time it will all make sense to you, incredible, incredible sense…." She said the problem was I wasn't ready. Soon I would be. I had only to go to the meetings, follow the reading list, read her paper again (she'd left me a finished copy).

"Promise you will?" she asked.

"Yes … I mean … yes, I think so…"

My husband smiled as he hung up the phone for me. "Finished with that little daydream?" he said.

I ignored this. I hummed a tune, as if the whole thing was of no concern to me. "I've got some studying to do," I told him.

"And what kind would that be? I hope you're going to take that Cervantes class I told you about. You really should be improving your Spanish so that you can begin to translate literature, instead of those reports you're always doing…. How much do you get paid for those things anyway?"

In the bedroom I could still hear him, but I pretended I was out of earshot. I glanced at the little brown suitcase sitting on our bed, so neatly packed, so compact. I couldn't bear to undo it. Instead I found room for it in our closet, behind the carton of shoes I still meant to give away.

"You know, I've been thinking…," my husband was standing in the doorway. "We really are due for a vacation. It's not going to be given to us—that's how it is when you freelance—we just have to take it. And we should, you know…."

For a moment I said nothing. And then, "Where would we go?"

"How about an island? Isla Mujeres? Or what about that new resort, Huatulco, is it?"

In the end we went only to Cuernavaca, just two hours away, but the hours in the sun were long and drinking Bloody Marys by the pool felt luxurious. I tried to imagine Karla in such a place, saw her in her long hair and dress, fidgeting with her rings: she would never sit so still. I was indulging myself in a way she wouldn't approve of. If only I'd brought one of the books she'd suggested; why hadn't I thought to do that?

Perhaps she knew; she did not write or call. Sometimes in the middle of doing something else entirely—going for a walk, speaking with my husband, even shopping—the image of the suitcase in our closet would suddenly interrupt my thoughts. I would see it clearly: its imitation leather, its contents so neatly packed, and for a moment I was on a plane somewhere, suitcase tucked under my seat; there would be no need to check such a small one.

His Sweater

I found his sweater on a rack in a store yesterday—
I mean, it wasn't his but it was the same sweater, the one
I used to wear when he forgot it in my room and I'd put
it on and smell his cologne and his baby skin, his thin
shoulders, his boy's body. Of course I bought it, even
though I haven't got much money—I mean I haven't
worked for over 3 weeks now—I tried it on in the store
and it was too big for me so I bought it because that's
how he wore it—with the sleeves rolled up at the wrists.
Anyway, it was a discount store so the sweater was half-
price. One of them was hanging above the rack for everyone to see—I wanted to take it down, to buy it and
hide the rest because it seemed like mockery, the store
having so many of them, his grey and yellow sweater
specked with blue. If only I had more money, I'd buy the
rest of them, buy all of them, but no, I wouldn't either—

they'd stare at me from the closet, or wherever I put them; there should only be one.

I'm wearing it now. It comes down past my waist and I let the sleeves dangle over my hands when I walk. It's my secret. No one knows why I wear it every day or anything about it; no one knows him here. I left him. I moved. It's winter and it's cold and I don't have a job, I'm still looking, but I've got his sweater on, nothing could keep me warmer.

My roommate, for instance, doesn't know much about me. But she knows I don't have a job. Of course when I moved in I told her I had one—I had to. Anyway I had money then. I don't anymore. I'm down to my last twenty that is. But there's still food in the cupboard. Most of it's hers, but some of it's my own. The can of chickpeas and tomato soup for instance. She asks how the job hunting is going. I don't let on that it's going very slowly. Today I saw a handwritten sign in a dark window: Help Wanted, Inquire Within. So I went in. It turned out to be the place where they make candy canes. The lady who interviewed me told me the work is very monotonous. You sit at a conveyor belt, see, and the candy canes are moving along it, except they're straight, they don't have a bend in the head yet, and that's your job, see, you take it and bend it while it's still hot. You wear gloves for the heat, also you have to work fast, you can't let them go by without bending them at the head. She said it's just a little wrist action, all day long, and would I be able to stand that? I said that I would. She decided to show me the factory, maybe to discourage me. There were women sitting all in a line bent over a conveyor belt just like she said. They were very quiet and they all wore plastic shower bonnets on their heads. The women were dark, they looked Mexican or Egyptian; she said I would be the only one who spoke English. She said with my talents and education why didn't I find a better job? I told her I couldn't. I'm sorry, she said, but I don't think I can hire you. Why not? My wrists are good, there's nothing wrong with my coordination. She smiled sadly. I'm afraid you wouldn't last here, is what she said.

I'm hoping this sweater will bring me better luck, though I'm aware that it's the color of my skin that's working against me. If only I were dark like those women … I can still see them, the way they stared at me when she brought me in the room; everyone glancing up at the same time, their eyes locking onto me, as if they thought she was bringing in the very person responsible for their misery.

I think I chose the wrong town. I'm not sure why I chose it after all. It's true I did a little research. I went to the local library; I looked in travel books, trying to find a city that would suit me. This one sounded the best of all, but it's very cold in wintertime, a kind of damp rainy cold that stays with you, even as you notice the rain has quit, leaving a faint sun which doesn't warm you. And then there's the fact that no one wants to hire me. They must sense that I'm not from here; in general they're very suspicious of out-of-towners. Unless you're from another country, I guess—thinking about those candy-caners.

Of course now I have no choice and am stuck where I am, having no money to relocate myself with. He doesn't know where I am. I did it all very carefully, dramatic-like almost, first investigating where to go, then not answering the doorbell when he rang, hiding behind the curtains so he wouldn't see me, not answering the phone. What a shock he must have had to find me gone! He didn't want me to leave him. But I had to. Maybe he'll find me here … but I left no traces. Unless there was something I did without knowing … but no, I purposely told no one, it was all as secret as a sewn-up pillow with none of the inseams showing.

Sometimes I wish—just for a moment—I had let something slip…. It would be nice to talk to someone I know, to reminiscence about everything … but I know that desire is dangerous, it's just giving in, exactly what I'm not supposed to do. Still, it's all very strange to me here, unlike where I used to live and my roommate doesn't in-spire confidence. I guess I feel guilty that I'm not out there job hunting—but nobody seems to want to hire me. Even though I'm down to my last twenty, I'm going to buy his cologne. I can get a small bottle for $9.95. I like the way it smells, it makes me feel supremely happy. I've already gone in the store and opened the flask five times, I know they don't want to see me in there again, but the next time I go in I'm buying it. But I've got to find a job … maybe they need someone at the perfume counter? I'm very tired, I feel sleepy all the time now. I'm going to sleep right now.

It's very cold here. I know I've said that before, but I can't seem to get warm enough, even with his sweater on all the time now. I guess I should have known, in a place where it rains rather than snows, the air is continually wet and grey and cold. When you walk along the street you meet no one's glance because everyone is looking down at their feet to keep the rain out of their eyes. These are things the travel book didn't let on. Of course (I tell my-self again), I should have known, a travel book is geared for tourists, not future residents. And it's strange to live with someone who barely talks to you—she's gone all day working and then when she comes home she goes into her room, closing the door behind her. I hear the TV come on and it stays on even as she falls asleep, sometimes with the light on. She must eat dinner somewhere else because I never see her cook, there's really no food in the house—is she afraid I'll eat it, that she'll have to invite me to share with her? Because she doesn't seem to want to have much to do with me, except for the rent money which I've got to find in a few weeks' time. What to do—?

Well, yesterday I really did try hard, even though I was tired after only three hours. I felt vaguely nauseated all day, kept thinking of my bed—a mattress only, but thick and soft, with cotton sheets and five blankets piled on to make a warm cave—could think of nothing else at times, though I kept on. And it was worth it I guess because I found a job. Hard for me to believe, even now, but someone said they would hire me. It's a Swedish bakery in what looks to be a Scandinavian neighborhood where once it was probably very popular, a fine business, only now there is a newer, much larger bakery just four blocks away. I'm to work the counter. Knowing a paycheck will be coming to me, I can afford to make a purchase, something I've had my eye on.

Today was my first day. There's a bus I can take to work that lets me off a block from the bakery; it was almost all filled with retarded children. They all smiled with big Hello!s as I got on the bus. One of them grabbed my arm—for a minute I thought he wouldn't let go—as I walked down the aisle. What kind of bus had I gotten onto? I kept staring at the driver, trying to get his attention; shouldn't he warn me the bus wasn't for me? But then others got on and no one seemed surprised, no one else stared at the kids the way I did; you could see it was normal and matter-of-fact to them, so I sat watching out the window, making sure I wouldn't miss 52nd Avenue, where my stop is.

It's a nice walk to the bakery past little garden plots, small shrubs of heather and other plants I don't recognize. The houses are all pale blues and pinks and yellows, it felt like Easter rather than winter with the sun finally shining. I felt happy, full of purpose for a change as I walked to my job.

What a very old cash register I have to use. You punch the numbers and the bell rings and it opens the drawer but it does no adding at all and I have to do the figures myself with pencil on a paper bag. The customers watch my addition very closely. Not that there are very many customers. There are long moments, hours I suppose, without anyone coming in, and even if someone comes in, they're usually just looking. Or smelling. They don't want the bear claws or Danishes or the Swedish Rye—all they touch is the day-old. There's a big tray of it and it's half-price and that's all anybody ever buys.

When there are no customers I go in the back to ice the bear claws and the Danishes. It's hot and the smell of icing sugar mingles with his cologne and the smell is sickly sweet and overpowering; I can smell it on his sweater long afterward. Sometimes I feel as if I'll faint and I lose my appetite even though I'm hungry but anyway, there's nothing to eat but Swedish pastry. The baker and I don't say much to each other. The owner told me he's just trying him out, he's a Vietnam Vet, he didn't have a home but now he's living out of a trailer. Let me know if he starts acting loopy on you, he's been hospitalized before. We don't bother each other. Every so often he goes out the back door to have a smoke and get out of the heat of the kitchen, I suppose.

The front bell tings and I go out to greet the customer and there's a man with long red hair and a strangely fitting suit, "Could I please have some crumbs to feed the birds?" "Crumbs…," I say, thinking where I'll find some. "You know, any leftovers, any day-old you can't sell, they just love that…." I hand him a bag of day old pastries. "The birds will be very happy … they'll thank you ever so much," he says in his slightly British accent.

It's raining again. Everything feels and looks the same now, as if all the colors have run into each other, to form one grey muddy blotch. The children smile and wag their heads at me as I get on the bus, the houses are the same ones day after day as I get off and walk past them, customers trickle in, the same white-haired men and women searching through the day-olds, then Mr. Crumbs arrives and I give him a bag and he tells me how much the birds liked what I gave him yesterday. The baker avoids me, grunting at me only when the bear claws are ready for icing, the owner stops by at the end of the day, complains about how little money we made and hints at closing the business. How slowly time goes. When I think it's only been a month since I came. I keep waiting, though I tell myself I am not, I know that underneath I am in a waiting state. I catch myself hoping that he'll come, that his face will suddenly appear through the dust of the bakery window, his smile revealing for a moment the way his front tooth crosses the one next to it, his eyes also widened in a smile of surprise.

One wonders why one covers one's tracks so well: why didn't I leave a trail of crumbs, even if Mr. Crumbs' birds found them? (Why isn't life more like a fairy tale?) What did he think when he rolled over and nothing was there to stop him, not even a depression, still warm in the bed, but the feel of the sheets, cool and empty—? And when he stood outside my door, pressing against the bell, when he looked up only to see the curtains drawn against him, when he let the phone ring into the dark of my apartment and no voice, no gesture, not even the sound of footsteps on stairs ever answered him. The truth is it was not love, though he said it was. He told me he loved me again and again, but I know otherwise.

I often gave him small tests and he never passed them. Once at a party his boss gave, I waited for him to introduce me to at least one of the many strangers and when he didn't, did nothing at all (I might as well have not been there), I stayed with the smallest member of the party, the boss's nine-year-old son, until even he deserted me. I fingered the canapés, sat in the space on the couch someone had vacated and waited for my lover, talking with great animation to the boss's wife, to find me.

He was angry after the party, asking what was wrong with me, why couldn't I show any interest, why did I have to sit in a corner talking to no one? Because you didn't care enough to introduce me. Then why did you disappear on me? We argued. He didn't understand that it wasn't me who had failed but him; he'd failed miserably. There were other tests as well and even the smallest ones he did no better on: the fact that he forgot my birthday, that you couldn't find any of the small presents I'd given him, any trace of me at all, in his bedroom. The last one of course was when I left him. He should have tried to find me; if you love someone you don't just let them slip through your fingers. But after three or four days he stopped coming by, the phone didn't ring; there wasn't even a letter from him. It was very disappointing to me, though it only confirmed what I'd already suspected....

There's a certain look in the nape of the neck, the way the hair is cut (he always kept his cropped short) that reminds me of him. I see it somewhere—the back of a boy on the bus, a man standing at a street corner waiting for the light to change—and my heart starts to hammer; it's him, I think, he's come to find me, he knew how to after all—and then the man turns and I see his face in profile, a nose too long, a forehead hidden by hair, and I realize how far I'm sinking.

Today I lost my way. Isn't it strange how you can walk the same path day after day to the point where you could do it blindfolded, you know it so well—and yet, maybe because of this, because you're no longer looking where your feet step or paying much attention as you sit on the bus to count two blocks after the white church and press the bell then, so the bus will hit your own stop in time— you've stopped paying attention to these signposts and milestones, thinking the world will take care of itself and you along with it. But it isn't so. You relax your guard and when you suddenly realize the bus has gone way past the white church, blocks and blocks (who knows how many) past your stop, you rush to get off and walk backwards, having no idea where you are or how to get where you need to go.

I was in a different neighborhood. The houses looked similar and yet something was off too—was it that the paint was peeling or that the fences were too high and unfriendly-looking? On the steps of one fenceless house a cluster of men sat. I thought of asking them directions, but the way they let off talking to stare stopped me. They seemed to know that I didn't belong, that there was no reason on earth for me to be walking down this stretch of sidewalk past their home, and I didn't feel like confirming this for them. I thought I should turn around, retrace my steps to the main avenue, but I'd been walking too long. I was sweating, even though the air was chill and sunless, and my heart was beating too quickly, bumping against my rib cage. I could feel a separate heartbeat, less distinct but just as rapid, within me. I knew this made no sense, that I was imagining things—I knew this, but I heard it even so: my own and another smaller beat right along beside it, a kind of childish echo. It made me walk faster listening to the chaos inside me; I hugged myself as I walked trying to get warmer—I was chilled and yet I was sweating. I don't know what I was thinking, my mind was all jumbled, I only heard the beating getting louder and faster, and I started to run, as if to outdistance it, to leave it all behind me in a heap on the pavement....

A woman was leaning over me when I came to. Are you all right? Can I get you to the doctor? Of course I refused, I was fine, but when she asked me where I lived, I told her 51 Dakota Street. "Dakota Street—where is that?" she asked, and I told her, "On the corner of Greene, right next to the laundromat...," before I realized that that was where I used to live. I tried to remember my new address, but my mind was numb, it kept refusing. She walked me to a bus, she kept asking if I was sure I didn't need a doctor, that maybe I was anemic or wasn't I pregnant, but I denied it.

When I got home I crawled into bed and stayed there. I dreamed he was lying beside me, his arms wrapped around me. He whispered that there was no one else but me, no one else he loved, even though when I'd walked by the Turkish restaurant one night I'd seen him with Catalina, a woman from work. It was only business he'd said when I confronted him, but I knew better: there were candles on the table. Other things came back to me as I lay sweating beneath my quilt, things I hadn't wanted to remember: the party he took me to where his friend confessed to us he used to sleep with his sister and I had to leave the room, I felt so sick to my stomach, the times he told me he wanted to marry me, that he wanted me to have his child, and I believed him, but when I came to meet him once at work I saw him leaving with Catalina. I followed them until they got into separate cars and I could no longer find them. It was hard to tell anymore what I was remembering and what I was dreaming as I woke up sweating and fell back to sleep again.

The woman who'd helped me on the street came in, round-faced with hair pulled back. She bent down to whisper in my ear, He's here now. I found him. I stared at her in astonishment. How did you know? How did you find him? And then he was there, just as he'd always been, his smile a warm one. I'm taking you home, he said. I held onto his arm as we walked out of the room. A flock of birds flew out from under our feet as we walked and Mr. Crumbs, his red hair all straggly, scolded us. You mustn't step on my birds! Be careful!

There's our bus, I yelled, and we ran to board it. But he reached the door before me. The bus didn't wait as he stepped inside; the steps folded up and the bus pulled away. I saw the children at the back window. Mouths and noses pressed against glass, they waved, their faces like waxed moons.

The Summer of Zubeyde

That was the summer I saw a man die. I think it was a heart attack; we were never really sure except that right before he died, he looked as if his chest was going to explode—he'd pulled off his shirt, tore it off actually, then stood, ripping, clawing at himself, until suddenly, with his face, his whole body the red of cooked crab shell, he fell backwards. We walked up to him as he lay on his back, his skin turning a darker shade of red, of magenta, of almost black—we stood back. Someone went to call an ambulance. There were small children watching with more curiosity than horror, their eyes wide, leaning against each other as they watched, and someone's mother told them to leave, to go on home, and I was surprised to see them do just as they were told. I looked back at the man on the sidewalk and realized I was still holding my heart, hadn't once taken my hand from my chest, as I watched life leave this man. And then suddenly he gurgled, bubbles of spit ran from his mouth and we saw his face was purple now and realized we'd heard his death rattle. The ambulance arrived soon after.

Even after they administered CPR (but he's already dead, we whispered among ourselves), placed him on a stretcher (it took all four of them to do that, his body had taken on the weight of stones), even after they took him away in the ambulance, sirens screaming, we stood, a small circle of women, rooted to the spot. I had been on my way to the elementary school where I was teaching English to recent immigrants—parents of school children—and it seemed strange that I would continue to walk, that I would stand in front of my students and pick up where we'd left off. Would I tell them I saw a man die? I realized I was still holding my heart. The crowd was reviewing the scene, "It was a heart attack, the way he tore off his shirt, like he was *burning up* inside—that's how it hits you." "Ain't it something, look how quickly a life can be taken away..." "Who was he? You think he lives around here? Do you think he was homeless—he had that plastic bag with him— what was in it?" "Who knows...." There was silence and still we stood there grouped around the spot on a side- walk in Brooklyn where a fifty-or-so-year-old white man had died among strangers.

Nothing marked the portion of the sidewalk, no blood, no stain of any sort, yet I knew I would remember it always, would think of it each time I walked to and from the elementary school, "This is the place I saw a man die...," and I did, saying it to myself each time I passed, as if the words gave meaning to his death, or to the fact I'd been among the few witnesses that hot summer afternoon in July.

There were other things I saw that summer without quite understanding. I saw a man jump out of his car and chase a small black boy, telling him to stop, then suddenly reaching for something in his waistband, pulling out a gun, aiming it at the boy, "So help me God, I'll shoot you if you don't stop...." The boy ran from him in crazy terror, zig-zagging his way past houses, trees, between cars, until the man only looked after him, swearing as he put away his gun, "Some little nigger boy think he can ruin my car ... think he's going to get away with that...," while I won-dered why the rest of us, spread out on opposite sides of the street, didn't attack him. But he had a gun, and his rage made him crazy and irrational, and we only stood there watching as he revved up the engine and tore off down the block.

They were things that seemed remarkable and yet I didn't know how to talk about them in all of their awful-ness; I was afraid I would diminish that part of it and so of course I never did tell my students, "I saw a man die...," or mention the crazy racist who cared more about his car than a child. I saw things that made me wonder what had brought me to that place at that time, but I said nothing to anyone and maybe that's why the events never quite left my mind, would come back to me: the gurgling last breath, the man aiming his gun, teeth clenched, "So help me God...."

It was a summer when events seemed just out of my grasp, like a film I was playing a part in—I'd been given a script in which no one's lines appeared but my own: I read them and believed them; I never even asked where they came from. But I was never sure where the film was headed, what anyone else's lines were—even who the other actors were. Sometimes I thought it was Zubeyde who held the key. It was the summer of Zubeyde—that's how I think of it now.

She was one of my students in the class of immigrant women that I taught. Only unlike the others, Zubeyde (her name sounded like Zoo-bay-da) was not the parent of a child, was not married, but had been invited to join the class by Fatima, I think it was. The women were from Kuwait and Saudi Arabia and Yemen—most of all, from Yemen. They were large and round and wore layers and layers of skirts, blouses, sweaters and headscarves—that's how I remember them, colorful in their wrappings, even though it was summer, a particularly hot and humid one at that. Only Zubeyde was different. Where they were round, she was quite thin, her dark hair cut short. And unlike the others, she always wore pants, straight-legged brown pants that seemed to accentuate her thinness. She wasn't beautiful, not remarkable, except for her eyes. Very large and quite black, her eyes exposed her. Her laughter and sadness collected there. But mostly she kept them downcast. She was so reserved, so awkward in her shyness, she was like a skinny black bird perched on a chair, alert but precarious; at any moment she might fly away. And yet she always came. I'd walk into the classroom and find her there, writing her name in pencil at the top of her notebook page: Z u b e y d e, each letter a soft line and curl. I'd say "Good Morning," and she would smile shyly, twist in her chair; I knew she was waiting for the others to speak up, to relieve her. They spoke more but her understanding was greater, and she often translated, her voice little more than a whisper—so the rest could understand me.

The class was difficult. I'd never taught a class so basic. I knew that some of these women could not read and write in Arabic, yet I was supposed to teach them how to do so in English. It was a struggle, but they were good-humored, laughing at my attempts to get them to talk. We mostly concentrated on vocabulary, as I tried to build a base for them to speak from. I remember thinking how clever I was: after we got through colors and articles of clothing, I asked them to name for me each item of clothing, along with its color, that they were wearing. Because they wore so many, the exercise took a long time, longer still because each item was greeted with a lot of giggling. I knew that I was asking them to be immodest, but they also seemed to enjoy it.

It is of course a different exercise that I remember most often. I had taught my students the names of various occupations, as well as of family relations, and it seemed logical to put the two together: "What does your father do?" or "What is (was) your father?"

I went around the circle as I always did and heard "farmer," "worker," "doctor," "carpenter." It was Zubeyde's turn. She shook her head. I repeated the questions, "What does your father do?"

Still she shook her head no.

"I'm sorry," I said. "He's passed away?" I paused, then, "What did he do before?"

Again she shook her head. I ignored the stress on her face: her worried look, the eyes she kept averted. Thinking it was vocabulary she was lacking, and seeing for some reason the image of a man plowing a field—the old way—with oxen and hand plow—I persisted, "What was your father?"

"I don't have father," she said to me, and I saw that she'd begun to cry. The other women smiled at me, a smile I knew to mean, "You should have realized, Zubeyde doesn't have a father, poor girl," while I tried—clumsily, inadequately—to apologize.

"It's all right, poor thing, the teacher didn't mean any harm by it," I thought Fatima was telling her as she patted her on the shoulder, told her to dry her eyes. Soon after Zubeyde left the room.

She didn't come back for the rest of the session; she didn't come the next day or the next week even. The class, which had always been difficult to teach, was suddenly much harder. How could I communicate without Zubeyde's translations? I didn't think I could face her empty chair. The other students were friendly with me, warm even, but I felt little sympathy. Their jovial natures, their slowness—everything about them now bothered me.

I'd hurt her—how could I have done that? I who understood her shyness? What had made me persist—so perversely, it seemed to me now—in unearthing her father? Why couldn't I have realized—? Yet I'd persisted with my silly line of questioning, insisted on uncovering him: the father who had never been there, or who once had, but had long since deserted her, rejected her. Whatever blackness I'd unearthed with my clumsy digging now followed her, enveloped her. I felt a physical pain—something stabbing me—when I looked at her chair.

I asked Fatima and the others about her, but they only shrugged, smiled, offered nothing. I struggled to come up with what to teach, but it was as if the script had been yanked away. The emptiness gnawed at me.

"How is the class going?" The principal would stop me in the hall, grab my arm, look at me searchingly. It was his baby, a free program he had raised funds for.

"Very well," I lied, "really well, in fact."

"That's great. We've got to teach those parents English, they have to be able to understand what goes on here…. I'm glad to hear it's going so well," he'd say, giving me one last look before heading to his office. And I'd nod again, find my way to the classroom.

Again I had to face her empty chair, the hard blank wood sitting in the middle of the classroom. No matter where I looked, or what I was teaching, her chair caught me.

Zubeyde … Zu-bay-da — I loved her name, the way it sounded. Sometimes I'd say her name and the image of a small black bird would come to me, the one from the Turkish or Russian folk tales I'd read as a child: the bird alights on a branch; it holds the secret, the golden ring or lost key that will shatter the unlucky curse—or the bird is actually the heroine herself, the princess or youngest daughter, caught by a spell and transformed—though only temporarily—into a blackbird.

I told myself if I had a child I would name her that: Zubeyde. It seemed unlikely I would ever have one, but it calmed me to think that I would, that I had already chosen a name for her and the name itself, the fact that I'd pass it on to someone I loved, seemed to offer atonement for what I'd done.

I spent a lot of time in my apartment, despite the heat, the fact that my air conditioning worked only barely. There were only so many things I felt I could complain to my landlord about: there had been the clogged bathtub drain, the leak in the ceiling, and in the winter, the faulty heating; I felt I had to make do. I bought two rotating fans and placed them at either ends of my bedroom.

Sometimes I'd get out of the shower and lie on my bed naked, droplets of water still on me, and let the fans cool me. For a few moments, I felt luscious. I imagined I was in bed in a steamy hotel in the Yucatán, the ceiling fan beating a rhythm overhead. It was a place I had gone with my boyfriend.

I thought of it for the place only; it wasn't that I wanted to be with him. I hadn't seen him since the end of May, for almost two months now. We had broken it off—a relationship with no real future. I had thought there was one, but when I found myself pregnant, I realized there wasn't any, had never been one, and not long after the abortion, we stopped seeing one another.

He had come with me, sat beside me in the pale pink waiting room until my name was called, waited with the other couples and men (why was everyone younger than we were?) while I lay on the table and underwent the procedure, trying not to feel anything: not pain, no ache, certainly not desire for what the discarded tissue might have been. He paid for the taxi we took back to my apartment in Brooklyn.

But in bed, taking codeine for the sharp cramps afterwards, I suddenly couldn't stand the sight of him. I wanted him out of my apartment. He'd rarely stayed the night—I'd always gone to his place—why should it be different now?

"Why aren't you leaving?" I asked him, and then, as forcefully as I could, "I want you to leave me." He thought it was from some codeine-induced delirium that I spoke to him, but I felt quite lucid in my pain: I never wanted to see him again. I took more codeine after he left, curled up in a fetal position in my bed and tried to enter a long dark tunnel of sleep from which I might not have to exit.

I woke of course; many times over. Sleep was a thin skin, not the heavy quilt I wanted.

Eventually he stopped calling, stopped trying to convince himself that he wanted the whole thing to continue. I was alone, again, which is what I'd wanted. But it was confusing to me. We hadn't seen each other every week, we weren't living together ... but I missed him. We'd gone out a lot—to films, restaurants, museums. And there had been that trip to the Yucatán. He was someone who didn't mind spending money. That appealed to me. My life was far more interesting it seemed to me with him than without him. But I couldn't bear to let him back in. He'd ripped something from me. And yet he'd never pretended to want a child. He'd always been quite clear about it: even the cries and screams of children on playgrounds seemed to offend him. Usually we walked the long way around the block to avoid the playground near his apartment. When I walked by one now I sometimes saw it as he did: a tangle of bullies and brats. At any moment a child would burst into tears; another would feel triumphant. Had his own childhood been so horrible? He wanted us to be adults in an adult world; he was good at that. And I missed it now: the novels we'd read aloud, the heated discussions we'd had after a film we'd seen (he liked it, I had not), the time in bed. He was really very good in bed. But then I reminded myself that the bed was nearly always his, not mine; it was too much for him to come to Brooklyn. And I had been accommodating. I liked Manhattan, liked his apartment, I didn't mind, I'd said.

But I did. In retrospect I minded terribly. I minded so much that I forced the door shut on him and decided not to reopen it. I had no desire to examine its contents, the resentment that would come tumbling out if I did. When I found myself reaching for the phone, his number already at my finger tips, presenting itself easily through the buttons: 212/489-6—, I made myself stop dialing, forced myself to blank out the rest. Only once I let it ring; the guards had been off duty I guess. It rang until his machine answered. A relief really. I could set up the censors again.

I forced the door shut on him, and what came tumbling into my consciousness, what constantly presented itself before me instead was the image of Zubeyde. She filled the space that had been freed by him. But it was as if my mind had got caught on a thorn, a jag; it hung there; it was impossible to tear it away.

Her disappearance plagued me. There had to be a way to get her back to class—something I could come up with. Or maybe she'd come on her own; I had hope still. Walking to the school along my customary route, crossing the sidewalk away from the spot where the man had died, I told myself: today she'll be there. Today she'll be sitting in her chair, eyes downcast maybe, but she'll be sitting there....

But she wasn't. I waited. I taught distractedly, my heart gone out of what had always been a challenge. The door would creak open, a latecomer—Zubeyde! But a rustle of skirts, or the click of high heels: it was Ismaya, it was Fatima; it was the teacher next door who needed an eraser.... I felt the pit in my stomach harden and sink deeper. Would I never see her again?

Yet I did see her. At night I caught sight of her: slipping between buildings in a foreign city, where streets were rain-streaked and cobble-stoned. I tried to reach her, but the city was strange and labyrinthine, the alleys and buildings dark. Zubeyde's thin figure was always just out of my grasp. And yet, there was the sense, in the dream and upon waking, that I would still catch up with her, have the chance to speak with her, to extend myself to her.

I got her address from the secretary in the school office. Should I write her? Visit her? I was undecided. And indecision crippled me. I kept thinking she would show up—eventually. And then suddenly it was the very last week of the Parents' English Program. Two more classes and it would be over. The grant was up; I would not be teaching there again.

The apartment was on Newkirk Avenue. I decided
to walk there. I would ask her simply: Why have you
stopped coming to class? We miss you…. I rehearsed the
lines; they sounded ordinary, I thought, not deranged….
It was not so irregular, I convinced myself, for a teacher to
call on her absent student.

I found the building, rang 14F. No one answered.
Perhaps it did not work. Or no one was home—a Wednesday afternoon…. I tried again, waited to see if someone
would walk into the building, someone I could slip in behind, maybe even ask: Do you know the young girl in
14F…?

But no one came, no one answered. I stumbled over
the uneven sidewalk, nearly bumped into a woman with
packages.

"Teacher! So happy to see you!" It was Ismaya, my
most learned and stylish student, with dark wavy hair and
red painted nails. "My house," she said, pointing to a brick
building about five doors down from Zubeyde's. "You
come in? Please?"

I nodded. Perhaps she would know about Zubeyde,
I had only to ask her. She led me, holding onto my arm
with her free one, as if she thought I would soon change
my mind, desert her. "It's here, you see? Not so beautiful." She led me up dark stairs to her apartment.

We sat at a table in a small room and she made tea for
me, "Very good tea, from Kuwait, here, you have it," and
she gave me a wrapped package of loose black tea. "Nice,
yes?" and she motioned me to smell it.

It did smell nice and the tea she made for me was
warm and sweet and good. Ismaya was telling me about
her house in Kuwait, so big, so many rooms, so many beautiful things, so much space for her children. I realized that
she'd been well off, wealthy even in her own country; here
she was starting from nothing. Her children weren't with
her; she'd left them with her mother in Kuwait, to be sent
for later. Leaving one's children behind in another country, even if temporarily, must be awful. The sadness of it

crept over me, and yet my mind was on Zubeyde—how could I ask Ismaya? At last there was a pause in her conversation and gestures.

"Do you know what happened to Zubeyde? Why doesn't she come to class?"

Ismaya shrugged, smoothed the tablecloth with her hand, looked at me blankly as if to say, "I don't know. And why should it matter?" They hadn't been friendly; they weren't even from the same country.

"I am so glad to have American visitor in my new house, my teacher!" she said suddenly and smiled at me, and I felt guilty for not being interested enough in her, grateful enough for the tea and package. "You come again? Please?" she implored me as I left and I said I would and thanked her again for her generosity.

I tried the bell to Zubeyde's apartment once more, then crossed the busy avenue. From the other side of the street I counted fourteen floors. Was her window the one with the curtain drawn? Or the one next to it? It was impossible to know. Still I couldn't leave the spot on the sidewalk, couldn't stop myself from squinting upward.

But the windows remained motionless, two eyes that were closed to me, the one with the curtains drawn, the other staring blankly. I took the long route home, crossing the street to walk the sidewalk where I'd seen the man die, not stepping around the spot as I'd always done, not avoiding it like the crack I would as a child (step on a crack, you break your mother's back), but instead planting my foot fully, firmly, exactly on the place his thick body had occupied, as if asking it to wash over me: the smell of warm and sticky blood, of something freshly dead.

Radio Disturbance

When a certain commentator came on her favorite radio news program, the one with the voice like velvet: soft, reassuring, yet at the same time poised and programmed—not as spontaneous as she sounded, Julia would listen for a moment, her mind crowded with images, memories, before she reached over and turned it off. The voice was exactly like her therapist's. Ex-therapist's. It could have been the very same voice and woman: chestnut hair in a soft perm, small frame, delicate features, feminine attire. She had sat, legs resting on a footstool, crossed at the ankles—small boots in wintertime, sandals in summer—while Julia sat opposite, sweating in her thrown-together outfits, her too-bright socks and ordinary glasses. Once she'd come in contact lenses, "You look like you've been crying...." "Oh no, it's my new contacts—they don't fit right. I have to go back...." Nothing fit right. Yet she did not return to the expensive, very handsome ophthalmologist (who'd kept her waiting, making her late for therapy, "Doctors usually run late," her therapist had said, scolding almost, as if Julia were naive for not realizing, for not counting on at least two extra hours). Instead Julia went back to wearing her glasses, hardly attractive, but at least they did not make her look like she'd been crying. She was sure her therapist wore contacts, wore them with no trouble at all. She was always poised, never ruffled, even with her feet on the footstool, toes peeking through sandals, and her questions....

"I don't know where to start today...," Julia would say as she came in, sat down, looking at her therapist for a clue, though her therapist did not usually offer one (it was not her job); her features stayed the same—perhaps an eyebrow raised, no more—Julia was on her own, as she always was, that was the point, after all. She was not supposed to get assistance as she fished the murky depths of her life to come up with something they could examine. She was sure her therapist had no murkiness at all: a husband and two children in a beautiful (she was sure) home in Connecticut. Things were always a mess for Julia. But that was the point, wasn't it? Otherwise, why have this weekly appointment? The weekly appointment had gone on for a number of years, it was a constant, and Julia had learned what was appropriate, though it did not come naturally. Divulgence and vulnerability. The system was alien to her; all her life she'd been taught not to divulge too much, not to appear vulnerable; all her schooling in self-control was slowly being undone now. Perhaps too slowly for her therapist who sometimes seemed impatient with her. But what did she expect? It wasn't easy for Julia, but surely she'd made some progress?

Once a month she received a handwritten receipt for payment and this was Julia's report card. She could read her therapist's opinion of her by the way she wrote Julia's name. On good days (she'd divulged more, cried perhaps), the "f" in her last name, Fielder, was a capital, straight and firm, clearly showing respect, while on poor days (she'd said little—or not enough—had been too unyielding), the "f" was lowercase, written quickly, even sloppily. She did not believe her therapist knew that her receipt-writing was a grading system; she could never realize how much Julia scrutinized her handwriting—but then again, perhaps she did? One day she announced there would be no more receipts; Julia did not claim the appointments for insurance purposes—so what was the point?

"But, but…" There was a point, and Julia tried to think of something reasonable, something with which to argue for keeping them. But no, she could think of nothing to save what might be the only tangible things she'd ever have from her therapist.

When the receipts stopped, there were her own checks that came once a month from her bank, her therapist's nearly inscrutable signature having endorsed them, but the signature—done so quickly, with so many years of practice—revealed little, nothing really. She did not bother keeping them. Not like the receipts which she bundled together; even now, seven years later, she knew exactly where they were: the bottom of her top-left desk drawer. They were there still: evidence of all those years and that schooling—what else did she have to show for it?

At the top of the receipt was printed her therapist's Connecticut address—was it in a dream that Julia had visited it? Or had it been actual? No, she couldn't have really done that: taken a train to the suburban town, walked the streets (afraid to ask) until she found 151 School Street (of course she could have oriented herself by the school all along). She couldn't have really done that, for that would have been abnormal, the action of a disturbed individual, and while she might have problems in her relationships, difficulty trusting others—men in particular—she knew she was not disturbed. Yet the house's exterior: white, three story, gabled windows, porch shaded by a large elm, was quite clear to her, an album photograph she could take out and examine again and again. And then were the sounds of the two boys in the backyard, fighting over a bicycle ("You rode it last time! It's mine!" "No, it's mine! Give it to me!"), their voices fading as she walked away, afraid someone—*She*, most likely—would emerge from the house, see Julia standing there. Julia hadn't really gone there, had dreamt it only, or vividly daydreamed it: the house, the street, the town, for what reason had she to journey from Manhattan on a commuter train that took almost two hours? Not a commuter, she, whose job in a downtown Brooklyn office was not so far from her own apartment.

She remembered how she first found out her therapist was someone's mom. When she'd begun therapy—in that little room with the hard office chairs where they'd started—Julia had assumed her therapist was single. After all, she herself was. But one day: a knock on the door, a note handed to her therapist, who upon reading it, turned to Julia, "My son's babysitter ... I need to call her." Julia had stared in astonishment (she'd heard "son's"—later, she found out—it was really "sons'"), tried to cover her shock; in any case, it wasn't hard, her therapist wasn't looking at her as she quickly left the room. Still, Julia had refused to believe her therapist was married, considered her divorced, a single mom; later she would find out this wasn't true, had never been true at all. And one evening (her session changed mid-week to a late appointment), she even saw him, his face—white, pudgy—hidden behind the magazine he was perusing, or pretending to be. (It had to be him—after all, who could have an appointment at such an hour?) He was waiting for Julia's therapist, his wife—but what had they done with the children? This preoccupied Julia throughout the subway ride to Brooklyn—had they left them with a babysitter? All day? Was her therapist neglecting her children for her practice? Her practice for her children?

The interior of the house was dark, wood-paneled, many-roomed. There were two separate studies—his and hers, both book-lined: one with psychology and literature;

the other, history, biography. A playroom of course, a yellow-bright kitchen, a master bedroom and a room with a bunkbed for the boys. This she knew to have dreamed only. For even if she had actually ventured to that suburban Connecticut town, found the street, the house number, she would never have gone inside. Not even looked in the windows. Because apart from the tremendous risk involved, what would that say about her? It was not something she'd do, though of course, a person could dream whatever she wanted.

She remembered that when she'd seen no car in the driveway or in the garage, she'd gone behind the house to try the backdoor (this was not the time she'd heard the boys in the yard). To her surprise, it opened. The door took her into a sort of back-of-the-kitchen pantry—a mud room, wasn't it?—and from there she'd found the kitchen, the twin studies, all of the other rooms. Quite suddenly she'd had to relieve herself, and so she'd tried the bathroom, then worried about the sound of flushing—but what other choice was there? And now she remembered her therapist telling her: when you dream of excrement, it means you're angry. But that was in a dream, and this was—no, this was a dream also. Was she angry at her therapist? And for what reason? In the house she did not know what she was looking for—was it anything at all? Perhaps only a sense of who her therapist really was, outside of the little room, shades of blue, in which they met to discuss Julia.

There had been something odd in the bathroom; she'd almost forgotten to remember it. On the bathroom wall: a beetle collection. Once alive beetles, still menacing-looking with their pincer-like feet and hard beetle shells. Blue-black wings, some greenish, others edged with orange, pinned in rows behind glass. The glass and its frame were dusty, the beetles themselves disintegrating, it seemed to Julia: some with legs detached, antennae missing. As a child she'd been given a paperweight with a real Monarch butterfly—wings spread—inside. What had happened to it? Looking around her therapist's home, she half-expected to find it, sitting on a dresser top among hair clips and jewelry, resting on a stack of papers.

There was little else in the home that seemed odd or unusual (in the hallway a few pictures of India, aging temples and goddesses with too many feet and arms). Everything was neatly arranged, nothing strayed from its placement. There must be a woman who came to clean—for how could her therapist find the time to do such tidying? Unless her husband got involved—was he that sort of husband? Sharing everything? Generous, pudgy, yielding? Thinking of him, she decided she must leave—no, she wouldn't try out the bed like Goldilocks, nor would she be surprised by the cleaning lady.

And this she *had* dreamed, even if the other had actually happened: she was standing at the top of the stairs, holding onto the mahogany banister when she heard a key turn in the front door, the heavy door being pushed opened…. Her heart clattered in her rib cage, as though a stack of china plates were rattling, teetering at the edge of a high shelf; at any moment the entire stack would come crashing to the floor…. There was a narrow door behind her as she faced the stairs; she turned the handle slowly—as much as possible under the circumstances—so as not to make even the slightest noise, then crouched under the lowest shelf of blankets, towels, carefully closing the door from inside. How long did she crouch there? She heard steps on the stairs, then some movement in the room next door—that would be the master bedroom, wouldn't it? Just one individual it appeared—it was *She*, or it was her husband, or perhaps the cleaning woman…. The footfalls sounded heavy, like those of a man—it must be the husband, she decided, and prayed he wouldn't suddenly have the need for a clean sheet or towel.

How long had she waited there? Time had no meaning in that small dark space. She remembered hiding in the closet of her childhood home so she wouldn't have to go the doctor—or was it the dentist? She hated the chair, the drill, being told when to rinse and when to spit—and she never seemed to open her mouth wide enough. "Wider, wider please! Even wider! That's a good girl…." In the end, her parents tired of looking for her and she herself fell asleep, the faint smell of mothballs in her nostrils. Is that what happened in this other house? In the cramped dark space, she'd suddenly become conscious. Had she been sleeping? For how long? She listened for sounds…. Nothing answered. Still she listened, her ear pressed against the closet door. The house seemed to be in a deep sleep itself, not the trace of a footfall or a whisper.

And so it was. When she emerged from the cramped, dark room—how good it felt, but how much it hurt too to again be standing, how difficult to straighten out her shoulder—she saw that it was dark both outside and in. Could it really be two in the morning, as the kitchen clock announced it was? She heard the breathing of heavy sleepers—how wonderful that they could all sleep so soundly, even as an intruder crept through the house, slipping out the backdoor from where she'd entered. She herself was not much of a sleeper. She often woke—just at this hour, in fact: 2 or 3 a.m., to find sleep suddenly impossible. She'd turn on the light and read (she had a stack of *Vanity Fairs* by her bed for this purpose: Princess Di, an interview with Keanu Reeves, Juliette Binoche—now there was a beauty—etc.). Or she'd pace her one-room apartment, walking from corner to corner, as if she didn't already know everything by heart, but sometimes things looked different in the middle of the night and she'd see something she hadn't noticed before: an odd figurine or a magazine she'd forgotten she'd taken from her therapist's waiting room—one she'd never buy herself, nonetheless, she was interested: *Lear's* or *Psychology Today* or something similar. Sometimes she made herself some warm milk with honey, a concoction she'd been told induced sleep. But nothing really helped. And then two or three hours later she'd drift off, and oh how very difficult it was to get out of bed when her alarm announced she had to, had to get ready for work; there were exactly thirty-two minutes to get to her cubicle in the office.

   She'd had to wait for the train, the 5:20 a.m., and then there was the fear that *She* would be on it—or her husband (Julia was sure he knew what she looked like, knew all about her; it was only natural after all to discuss such things—one's job—over dinner). But the 5:20 a.m. for a working Mom—when would she see her children? It was much too early for her therapist to be journeying to Manhattan, Julia decided; it would mean she really *was* neglecting her sons for her practice, when Julia was convinced it was the other way around: she was neglecting her practice for her sons. When she told her therapist, for example, about Anders, the new manager—he was from Denmark and had a wonderful accent when he spoke English; he was very refined, handsome, in a dark ungermanic way—when she told her therapist about this new relationship (because it was becoming one, hadn't they bumped into each other on the subway, and how much of an accident could that have been?), how could she be sure her therapist wasn't thinking about her sons— whether they'd eaten a proper breakfast, that she should have given them whole milk, or least 2%, rather than skim—how could Julia be absolutely sure she wasn't thinking these things?

   There was of course no way to be. But there were hints, signs: when Julia was describing Anders, for example, her therapist suddenly interrupted her, "What's wrong with your shoulder?" Julia had been shrugging her right shoulder, as if to get a cramp out of it—but what did that have to do with anything? She didn't want to talk about it, and wasn't she supposed to set the agenda around here? Wasn't that the point of the whole enterprise? "I was talking about Anders...," Julia said—surprised, offended—and reiterated how much the relationship meant to her. Her therapist sighed, then said, "It's a minimal relationship, like so many of your other ones...."

   How could she have made a remark like that? Hadn't she heard Julia telling her about the card she'd found for him, especially for him—it had a picture of an angel (she had joked that Anders was really an angel; he wore his hair in a thin ponytail, just like the angel-men in a Wim Wenders film, and he'd gotten the joke—he'd laughed, had appreciated it deeply). How was this "minimal"? There was an explanation, of course, a very simple one: her therapist's mind was on her children—what she'd put in their lunchboxes, how she'd have to remind the older one not to bully, the younger not to pick his nose in public places.

Julia was sure that it was her therapist's pessimistic attitude which had colored her relationship with Anders—it had started off so promisingly, and then suddenly he was mentioning his wife whenever he could, "My wife was just saying this morning..." Julia couldn't hear the rest; her ears stung. Since when did he have a wife? (No, she hadn't noticed the ring on his finger; she wasn't in the habit of paying attention to such things). When she told her therapist, there was that look again: "Uh-hmmm, I told you...," was what her eyes said. But what did she know about it? Julia was sure she'd missed at least half of the Anders incidents she'd just been describing to her, missed all sense of coincidence, the subtleties in the relationship.

It was around this time that Julia considered leaving therapy. She figured she'd have X-amount more money each week to spend or to save—to assist in scraping by was more like it—and the pessimism which had recently settled like a mist, fogging up all her dealings—particularly with men—might begin the business of lifting. She wondered how best to announce her intentions. It was difficult after so many years; would her therapist think she'd made enough progress? Julia considered that she had—in any case, the whole enterprise recently seemed to be blocking her; by ending it, she would at least be eliminating any possible impediments. She was wondering how best to explain this, to justify her departure—of course, financial considerations were no small matter, either, though a therapist might not agree with this—when quite suddenly, out of nowhere, her therapist announced she'd be switching her practice to Connecticut. She would not be making the commute any longer—thus they needed to think about bringing Julia's sessions to a close. She had the name of a therapist who'd be willing to take Julia on—a man, actually, someone who could be very beneficial in the process....

Julia stared at her in astonishment. But why protest when she herself had been considering closure? "That's very interesting," she finally said, "because actually, I myself was thinking about ending..."

The look on her therapist's face, a sort of Come-now-you-aren't-going-to-be-that-defensive-after-all-this-time expression stopped her from going further.

"But it's true...," Julia began again, then stopped, unsure how to continue.

"How do you feel about my leaving?"

Julia said something to the effect that she recognized her therapist's sons were her priority, that of course she must want to spend more time with them, and with her husband in their beautiful home in Connecticut—

"Yes, but how does that make you *feel*?" was the question again, and Julia couldn't think about how it made her feel, except that her right shoulder was cramping up on her again, something that had not happened in a long while. ("You should see a chiropractor," Anders had said—that was when they'd shared thoughts, feelings—but she never did). "I don't know," she finally said. "My shoulder hurts...."

"Well, yes," her therapist said, "we never did talk about that shoulder...."

"Well, it's odd—" Julia answered, thinking she might explain it. "It was just a dream, but you know, it hurt the next day as if I'd actually done it..."

"Done what?"

"Oh you know, hidden in someone's closet..."

"No, I don't know ... whose?"

"Oh, it could have been anyone's ... anyone's linen closet at the top of the stairs, with beige and gold bath towels and washcloths, and clean sheets folded on the lowest shelf...." (Julia was making an educated guess, for in the dark how could she have seen these things?) She described the contents further—the color of the sheets, for example—then interrupted herself, "There," she said, "It doesn't hurt anymore—it's gone. I feel fine now."

She thought her therapist looked puzzled; the look was in any case long enough to include a mental inventory of a hall closet.

"I feel better now, much better," Julia repeated, "I'm sure that I'm ready to move on."

And that's how it had ended, more or less—there hadn't been much more than that (something more about closets, she remembered, about the one in her childhood home; she regretted having referred to it). And then it was over. So many years ago—seven to be exact. She had a different job now—in Manhattan, not Brooklyn; she even had a steady relationship, though they weren't ready to move in with one another. She still rented the same one-room apartment, still woke up—more often than not—at 2 a.m.; this was how she'd gotten attached to the early morning news program; in fact, she was listening to it now. But had she wasted time—and money—in therapy? Because it seemed to Julia—as she listened to the velvet-voiced commentator come on (instinctively she reached over and turned the radio off)—that if her therapist's attitude had been more positive, more *accepting*, Julia might be with Anders now—he could have left his wife, he couldn't have been content with her (or that cramped Queens apartment—who would have guessed he lived there? Dark and dingy with moldy wall-to-wall carpet?). They could have lived anywhere—maybe even Denmark, she wouldn't have objected—could have quit their jobs and traveled, lived out of backpacks, or wheel-along suitcases—why not? At the time so much had felt possible.